Plastic
Polly

Also by Jenny Lundquist

Seeing Cinderella

Plastic Polly

JENNY LUNDQUIST

ALADDIN M!X
New York London Toronto Sydney New Delhi

ALADDIN M!X
Simon & Schuster Children's Publishing Division
1230 Avenue of the Americas, New York, NY 10020
First Aladdin M!X edition March 2013
Copyright © 2013 by Jenny Lundquist
All rights reserved, including the right of reproduction
in whole or in part in any form.
ALADDIN is a trademark of Simon & Schuster, Inc.,
and related logo is a registered trademark of Simon & Schuster, Inc.
ALADDIN M!X and related logo are registered
trademarks of Simon & Schuster, Inc.
For information about special discounts for bulk purchases,
please contact Simon & Schuster Special Sales at
1-866-506-1949 or business@simonandschuster.com.
The Simon & Schuster Speakers Bureau can bring authors
to your live event. For more information or to book an event contact
the Simon & Schuster Speakers Bureau at 1-866-248-3049
or visit our website at www.simonspeakers.com.
Designed by Mike Rosamilia
The text of this book was set in Mrs Eaves Roman.
Manufactured in the United States of America 0213 OFF
2 4 6 8 10 9 7 5 3 1
Library of Congress Control Number 2012936752
ISBN 978-1-4424-5248-0
ISBN 978-1-4424-5249-7 (eBook)

To my parents, Thomas and Pamela Carroll.

I have never doubted your love.

Chapter 1

✰　✰　✰

True Confession: Every time I hear someone call me Plastic Polly, I imagine myself slowly turning into a life-sized Barbie doll, one phony piece at a time.

I'M STANDING IN FRONT OF MY EX–BEST FRIEND, ALYSSA Grace. She's on the other side of the salad bar, scooping for a cherry tomato that doesn't want to be caught. Looking at Alyssa, you'd never know how stubborn she is—she's so tiny and slight, her thin white-blond hair wisping around her face, that it seems like the slightest brush of wind could knock her over. But Alyssa can hold a grudge as deep and thick as the roots of the old maple tree in my backyard.

I haven't spoken to Alyssa in over a year. Not since the first week of seventh grade, when she ditched Kelsey and me. We ignore each other in the hallways and at football games and dances. But today I want to tell Alyssa the truth: that I miss her. That having only one best friend—instead of two—has left me feeling lopsided.

My two friends next to me, Melinda Drake and Lindsey McCoy, don't notice I've frozen. They're still chattering about the banners for Groove It Up we posted all over campus this morning.

I spear the cherry tomato with my fork and drop it onto Alyssa's plate. "Here." I flinch because my voice sounds squeaky—the voice I used to have in sixth grade when I got nervous. Not like my voice now—the one I practice every day in the shower.

Alyssa looks up at me, and I hold my breath, wondering if she'll walk away. But instead, she gives me a tentative half grin. I smile back and try to think of something to ask her. If she still takes voice lessons from that old woman who never brushed her teeth—we used to call her Lady Onion Breath. If she still goes to thrift shops. If she still eats chocolate ice cream with crushed-up pretzels.

Before I can say anything, Melinda, who thinks our popularity is a license to be nasty, snaps at Alyssa, "Hey, you with the hideous hair and unibrow. Can you move, already? The rest of us would like some tomatoes too."

Alyssa doesn't look at Melinda, but from the way her

knuckles whiten around the salad spoon she's clutching, I know she heard. And whatever chance I had to talk to her slips away.

The half grin on Alyssa's face twists into a sneer. "Hey, Plastic Polly. How's it going? Heading over to Fakeville?"

Several students turn and stare at us, and I feel my face flush. Sure, I know half the school calls me Plastic Polly behind my back. But no one ever says it to my face. And hearing it from Alyssa, it feels worse. Like a sharp stab in the back—especially since it was Alyssa herself who invented the name.

If Alyssa had said it when we were alone, I could have let it go. I could have apologized for what Melinda said, could have asked Alyssa all about her life and hoped she's not still mad at Kelsey and me. But too many people are watching us. And after all, I am a member of the Court. We don't apologize.

I lift my chin and stick a hand on my hip. My other arm drops gracefully to my side, and my arm bracelets jangle to my wrist. I look confident. In command.

I know this because it's a move I've practiced a million times in front of the mirror.

In my best haughty voice I say, "Do you mean over there?" I point to the Court—the table where the popular kids sit—and nod. "We're talking about Groove It Up, but if you hate us so much, maybe you shouldn't bother trying out."

The minute the words leave my mouth, I regret them. Groove It Up is a talent show competition between Winston Academy and our rival, American River Middle School. It is *the* social event of the fall, and it's always planned by members of the Court. This year is an even bigger deal than usual, because it's the competition's fortieth anniversary and the winning school will receive two prizes. First, the members of the school's Talent Team will get to perform on *Good Morning, Maple Oaks*. And the entire school will be treated to a private concert by Shattered Stars. They're a really popular band whose members all grew up here in Maple Oaks. They're too famous to play in small towns anymore, but somehow the city council talked them into it.

I posted the sign-up sheet for tryouts this morning before school started. After first period I went to check on it and saw Alyssa's name written at the top. Alyssa has an amazing voice, and when we were in Winston Academy's elementary section—when we were still friends—she would tell Kelsey and me how she couldn't wait to grow up so she could become a famous singer. She must be dying to land a slot on the Talent Team, hoping we'll win and she'll get to be on TV.

Alyssa's face crumples, but then her expression quickly hardens and she raises her voice. "So you're saying the try-outs are rigged? Only the Court suck-ups have a chance?"

Now more people are staring at us. "What? No, of course not." Although—and I would never admit this to Alyssa—in a way the auditions *are* rigged. Kelsey, my best friend and this year's PlanMaster, has decided the cheerleaders, who are so good they won the state championship last year, will make up half of our Talent Team. She'll break the girls up to perform in groups of two or three and then bring them all together for our final act. So even though tryouts haven't even happened, half the slots are unofficially taken. Kristy Palmer, captain of the cheerleading squad, has been practicing with her girls for weeks. I told Kelsey that seemed to me like allowing the star player of a baseball team to bat in every inning.

"Polly, Melinda, Lindsey!" Kelsey calls from across the cafeteria. "Get over here!"

Alyssa smirks. "Later, Plastic. Your master is calling you."

I scoop up my cafeteria tray, shoot Alyssa an irritated glance, and follow Melinda and Lindsey over to the Court.

The Court is a long rectangular table in the middle of the cafeteria. Directly above the table is a skylight—so the sun can shine down upon the chosen few of us who are allowed to eat there. Winston tradition dictates that the most popular eighth graders sit at the Court, as well as a few seventh graders who will take our place after we graduate.

Normally I get a small thrill as I approach the Court. I know it's not cool to admit this, but I adore feeling everyone's eyes on me as I saunter over to my usual spot. Outwardly I pretend to be bored, like it's no big deal. But inside I'm *loving* it. Especially when I catch people like Jenna Huff—who used to laugh at me and make fun of my squeaky voice when we were in Winston's elementary section—watching me.

It makes me feel like, *Ha! Look who's laughing now!*

Today, though, I can't bring myself to sit down right away. I take a detour to the condiment area, where I fill up tiny plastic cups with my four favorite salad dressings. I like to drench pieces of lettuce in the dressing. I call it salad fondue. Out of the corner of my eye I watch Alyssa. I'm hoping she comes over. Maybe then I can apologize.

"Hey, Polly." I look up and see Kate Newport, a girl who likes to hang around Kelsey and me, hoping we'll invite her to the Court. She's wearing a white tank top and a pink flippy skirt. It looks *exactly* like the outfit I wore to the pep rally a few weeks ago, when Kelsey announced she'd selected me as her Vice PlanMaster.

"Like my outfit?" Kate says.

"Um, sure. That's a super cute . . . necklace you're wearing." And it is. It's a small pink-and-white rhinestone medallion on a silver chain.

Kate smiles like she just won the lottery. "Really? If you like it, you can have it." In a flash the silver chain is dangling from Kate's finger, the medallion ticktocking above my salad.

"No, Kate, really. That's sweet, but I don't want your jewelry. Put it back on." I push the necklace toward her just before it dips into my salad dressing. "Please."

"Okay, but here's a bracelet. It'll look good with the ones you're already wearing." Kate thrusts a silver bangle at me. "Friends share, right?"

"Um, sure." I stick the bracelet onto my wrist. "I'll give it back to you tomorrow."

"Oh, no. Keep it. It's yours," Kate says, and practically skips away.

Here's the thing about being popular: Sometimes popularity is like your own personal good luck charm, a talisman that bestows favor, whether it's a bracelet, fifty holiday grams from people you barely know, or guaranteed invites to all the middle school events.

I glance over at Alyssa again. She's finished up at the salad bar and starts over to the condiment table. When she sees me, she changes direction and plunks down at an empty table just behind the Court. I sigh and look away.

But here's the other thing about popularity: It doesn't come cheap. Sometimes it makes you choose one best friend over another. And you can never admit to anyone that sometimes you wonder if you made the wrong choice. Because if you admitted that, they'd just laugh and say, "You're popular. What problems could *you* possibly have?" So instead, you keep your mouth shut, stick a fake smile on your face, and pretend you don't have any. Problems, that is.

It's just easier that way.

"Polly!" Kelsey hollers. "Are you keeping vigil over there, or what? I have an important question to ask you!"

With one last look at Alyssa, I turn away and head to the Court.

And stick a fake smile on my face.

Chapter 2

✿　✿　✿

*True Confession: No one at school ever told me
I was pretty until after I became popular.*

"FINALLY," KELSEY SAYS WHEN I TAKE MY USUAL SEAT at her right side. As the most popular eighth grader at Winston Academy, Kelsey sits at the head of the Court. "I need you to settle a disagreement between Melinda and me."

Everyone sitting at the Court—which today includes a few football players, Kristy Palmer and a couple of other cheerleaders, and Kelsey's soccer teammates—turns to stare at me.

"Okay. What is it this time?" Lately Melinda has been saying we should have certain rules at the Court, like Monday you have to wear pink, or Friday is jeans day, but

Kelsey—who never wants to be like anyone else—thinks it's a stupid idea. And when it comes to clothes, neither of us trusts Melinda. She's great at selecting an insult but less accomplished when it comes to fashion. Today Melinda's wearing a bright yellow sundress with brown polka dots, and frankly she looks like a talking banana.

Kelsey flips her long hair, which is as black and sleek as a panther's mane, over one shoulder and says, "Melinda thinks we should all wear the same costume to Kristy's Halloween party, but I say no way. What do you say?"

"Come on," Melinda begins. "The party isn't for a few weeks, and—"

"I already bought a costume," I say, cutting her off. "And there's no way I'm taking it back." I'd take Kelsey's side even if I hadn't already bought a costume. When you've been best friends since kindergarten, that's just what you do.

Kelsey grins triumphantly. "See? Two against one. Too bad, Melinda."

Melinda stabs at her salad and grumbles. "It's not fair. Just because you have a best friend who—"

"What was that?" Kelsey cocks an ear.

Melinda looks up and suddenly seems to realize everyone is looking at her. "Nothing."

Melinda changes the subject and begins talking about a reality show she saw on TV last night, but I don't pay attention. I'm looking over her shoulder, at Alyssa. In the window behind her several red and gold leaves from the maple trees drift slowly to the ground like lazy sailboats. I remember how Alyssa's dad used to pay me and Kelsey and Alyssa a penny for every leaf we picked up in their front yard. Kelsey and Alyssa always fought over the red ones.

"Earth to Polly," Kelsey says. "What's with you today? You seem distracted. And you took forever at the salad bar."

"Some girl was giving Polly a hard time." Melinda points her fork at me. "And Polly was just taking it." Melinda's voice is disapproving, like she's tattling on a small child who's just done something very naughty. Sometimes I catch her staring at me with a puzzled, distasteful expression on her face, like she can't figure out how I became popular. And lately Melinda's been taking her chronically cranky mood out on me—especially when she feels like me and Kelsey are ganging up on her.

Before I can remind Melinda that I did stick up for myself (and still feel bad about it), Kelsey says, "That's your problem, Polly. You don't assert yourself. Someone messes with you"—Kelsey pounds her fist on the table—"you squash them."

"Squash them?" I laugh.

"Like a bug. And anyway, what girl was giving you a hard time?" She turns to survey the cafeteria, eyes narrowed.

"Some ugly girl from my history class," Melinda says. "She's no one."

"Her name is Alyssa," Lindsey says. "She's usually pretty nice." Lindsey quickly glances at Kelsey and me, to see if she said the wrong thing. As a seventh grader Lindsey is careful to stay on everyone's good side. So I smile back at her to let her know everything is fine.

Kelsey pales, and after the conversation turns to another topic, she leans over and whispers, "Alyssa Grace?"

It sounds weird to hear Kelsey use Alyssa's last name. Like she's a stranger. Like Alyssa isn't the girl we once bought special best friend necklaces with—a heart split three ways.

"She's sitting behind Melinda," I whisper.

Kelsey turns, and we both watch Alyssa. "Why is she sitting there?" Kelsey whispers. "Doesn't she usually eat lunch with her choir friends?"

"Yes."

Kelsey and I glance at each other—both of us silently acknowledging that, even though we don't talk about Alyssa, we've kept track of her the past year.

"Um, Kelsey?" A girl I don't know—a seventh grader, I think—tentatively steps forward. "Mr. Fish says he needs to see you. R-right now." Sweat breaks out on her upper lip, probably because she was forced to approach the Court without an invite.

Mr. Fish is the teacher adviser for Groove It Up. He seems nice enough to me, but Kelsey can't stand him. She gives a long-suffering sigh before leaving.

Afterward I get drawn into a conversation about the upcoming football game, and whether I think the Winston Wildcats will win on Saturday. I smile and nod, since I'm expected to care, but the whole time I'm watching Alyssa.

Sometimes I wonder what life would be like if the ground hadn't shifted, elevating Kelsey and me—turning us into middle school royalty—while Alyssa was thrust to the bottom of the middle school heap. Back when the three of us had sleepovers every Friday night at Alyssa's house, Kelsey and I would sing off-key to stupid pop songs on Mr. Grace's old karaoke machine. Every now and then Alyssa would join in—overpowering us with her diva voice. But usually she'd make funny faces and dance crazily around the room—like a chicken doing the hokey pokey— and we'd all laugh till we fell to the floor in hysterics.

"Hey, Pretty Polly," says Derek Tanner, a football

player sitting next to Kristy. "I'm going to get a soda from the vending machine. Want one?"

I nod and tell him thank you. In the past couple weeks Derek's started showing up at my locker, buying me sodas during lunch, and insisting on carrying my backpack in between classes.

After he leaves, Kristy and Melinda giggle, and Lindsey whispers, "He *totally* likes you."

"Maybe." The girls are convinced Derek has a crush on me, but I just can't get all that excited about it. I mean, yeah, Derek's really cute. But he also has this weird look on his face all the time—like he's constantly surprised by the smallest things. Plus, he smells like cardboard. Don't ask me why.

Also, I happen to know (since he mentions it at least once a day) that Derek is trying out for Groove It Up and really wants a slot on the Talent Team. If it weren't for the fact that Kelsey intimidates most of the boys at Winston, I think Derek would be buying *her* sodas. You know, go straight to the top, and all that.

I watch while Derek lingers in front of the soda dispenser, scratching his head and looking baffled—like the machine's playing a practical joke on him. Then I turn to the girls. "What if he only likes me because I'm on the planning committee?" I ask. "Or because I'm popular?"

"So what?" Melinda looks genuinely confused.

After that, Kristy tells us about the camping trip she went on with her family over the weekend.

"That sounds super fun," I say, watching Alyssa while I talk. "I love camping."

Melinda turns to me. "Didn't you tell Kate Newport last week that you'd rather stick a needle in your eye than go camping?"

"What?" I turn my attention back to the girls. "Oh, um . . ." Okay, I did say that. I wasn't trying to be totally fake to Kristy or anything, but I've noticed people sometimes get upset when you disagree with them over the smallest things. Like if someone says, "I really like lemon drops," and you say, "I don't like lemon drops," the other person gets all offended. Like you've just said you don't like *them*.

So in my opinion it's just easier to agree with people.

"Um . . . I forgot," I say.

"Hey, hey, hey, it's the PlanMaster herself!" says Toby Markowitz, another football player, as Kelsey plunks back down in her seat. "Death to American River!"

Then Kristy and the other cheerleaders start clapping and break into a chant, "WIN-ston! WIN-ston! WIN-ston!" I can't help it. I look around at the rest of the cafeteria and watch everyone else (including Alyssa) watch us. It feels good.

"Free concert with Shattered Stars, here we come! American River doesn't stand a chance with Queen Kelsey as the PlanMaster!" Lindsey says.

(Yep, Kelsey also has a nickname that we think came from Alyssa. The difference is, Kelsey *likes* hers.)

"It doesn't matter who the PlanMaster is," Kelsey says, rubbing her temples. "What matters is which school has the most talent."

"Stop being so modest," Melinda says, in a voice so sugary I wonder if *she* practices in front of a mirror. "We all know that if Winston wins, as PlanMaster, Kelsey should get all the credit." Melinda smiles, but her yellowish-brown eyes—that remind me of greedy wasps—don't. For a second I wonder if Melinda believes the opposite. If Winston loses, does Kelsey deserve all the blame?

I think Kelsey must wonder the same thing, because she snaps, "I *know*, Melinda. Okay? Since you remind me practically every hour."

Derek returns, having finally outsmarted the vending machine. He hands me a soda, and then offers one to Kelsey. "Here you go, Madame PlanMaster."

"It's dented." Kelsey turns the can to show Derek.

"Oh, yeah," Derek says, looking vaguely surprised. "I guess I dropped it."

"Look what I found." Kristy holds up an American River flyer advertising Groove It Up. "They hung it up outside of Chip's. Can you believe that?"

Groove It Up is a big deal in Maple Oaks, and a lot of the local businesses get into it, supporting one school or another. Chip's, the diner across the street from Winston, is always firmly on our side.

"Give me that." Melinda snatches the flyer, wads it up, and tosses it behind her. It lands in Alyssa's tomato soup, sending red liquid splashing onto Alyssa's face—which sends half the Court into hysterics.

"She looks better that way." Melinda gasps, laughing so hard she can't catch her breath.

Everyone goes back to cheering for Winston. No one notices that Kelsey and I aren't laughing. Alyssa, meanwhile, wipes the soup off with a napkin, revealing a face that's still tomato-colored. Then she hastily gathers her things. After she's cleared her tray, she starts for the staircase leading to Winston's lower level—the Dungeon, as it's known around campus.

"I want to go talk to her," I whisper to Kelsey.

"Absolutely not. She made her choice."

I turn and stare at Kelsey. "I wasn't asking for your permission."

I stand up and start after Alyssa. Behind me I hear Kelsey say, "All right, Polly. *Fine.* Wait for me."

I'm at the edge of the staircase, and Alyssa is down the stairs—heading into the Dungeon—when I call down to her, "Alyssa!"

This is the part I will always replay in my mind:

1. Alyssa turns to stare up at us.
2. Next to me I hear Kelsey pop open her soda, and icy liquid sprays my shoulder as the soda spurts everywhere. Then I hear a dull thud as Kelsey drops the can.
3. Alyssa grins, but her look quickly turns to panic and she mouths the word *No!*
4. I turn just in time to see Kelsey trip over the can and go toppling down the stairs, her screams tumbling after her.
5. When Kelsey lands, Alyssa is at her side.
6. Alyssa looks up at me. Then, like a mirror image, we each bring a hand to our neck.

Both of us reaching for a heart necklace that isn't there anymore.

Chapter 3

✫   ✫   ✫

True Confession: Besides Kelsey, I never show my report card to the girls at the Court. I don't want them to know I get straight As.

THIS IS THE STORY OF HOW I BECAME POPULAR AND LOST a best friend, all in the same week:

On our first day of seventh grade, Alyssa and I sat together at a side table in the cafeteria, trying to calm down Kelsey, who was livid that some eighth grader named Amanda had dared to call her Squirt in the hallway.

"It's not a big deal," Alyssa said. "And who cares what she says, anyway?"

"*I* care, Miss High-and-Mighty," Kelsey snapped. "And so should both of you. Do you know what kinds of decisions are made in the first weeks of middle school?

Where you sit, who you hang out with? It defines your entire existence."

"Okay, now you're just being overdramatic," Alyssa said.

"Don't talk to me about being dramatic, Miss I'm-Saving-My-Voice-for-Choir-Tryouts-Tomorrow." Kelsey stared pointedly at the scarf Alyssa had tied around her neck.

I kept quiet, but I actually agreed with Kelsey. Right then in the cafeteria most people (except for Amanda) seemed pretty nice—spread out like pieces of a living puzzle, trying to figure out where they fit. But eventually, I knew, everyone would find their matching pieces and connect together, making up Winston Academy's student body. After that, if you tried to switch groups or sit at a different table, people would look at you funny.

"If we were sitting at the Court," Kelsey said, "no one could touch us. We should go over there."

I'd only been a middle schooler for approximately four hours, but I'd been hearing all about the Court—the table where the cream of the crop of Winston Academy sat, ruling from on high—for years in Winston's elementary section. Jenna Huff always acted like it was just a given that she'd end up at the Court. Once, in fifth grade, I heard

Jenna and her friends making a list of the people they'd allow to eat with them once they were in charge. My name wasn't on it. "Polly's too dorky to sit at the Court," I'd heard Jenna say to her friends. But I wondered if the real reason was because every week I beat Jenna for first place in the class spelling bee.

Alyssa stared at Kelsey like she'd just suggested we chop off a finger or two. "You can't be serious. You have to be invited to the Court. No one just goes over and sits down."

"Oh yeah?" Kelsey stood up. "Watch me."

"Kelsey, wait!" I said. Alyssa and I grabbed our lunches and scrambled after Kelsey, who marched straight over to the Court and pointed to two empty chairs at the end of the table.

"Sit down," she commanded.

Alyssa and I sat. Kelsey dragged over another chair. Then she sat down and quietly began eating her lunch.

Meanwhile, everyone else at the table stared at us. Amanda, the girl who'd insulted Kelsey earlier, said, "What do you think you're doing?"

Kelsey smiled back at her. Then she proceeded to utterly pick apart Amanda's outfit and all the ways it wasn't worthy to be worn at the Court. When Kelsey finished, there was a stunned silence.

Until Brooklyn Jones, the most popular eighth grader, said, "What's your name?" After Kelsey answered, Brooklyn smiled and said, "Nice outfit." Then her smile vanished. "And, Amanda? She's right. Tomorrow don't bother sitting here unless you can clean yourself up. You're making us all look bad."

While everyone talked about clothes and football and their classes, I quietly ate my lunch and read an invitation I'd received in homeroom to take the Star Student test—a program for academically gifted kids. The students who passed the test were bused over to Maple Oaks High School during lunchtime to take a couple of afternoon prep classes. I hadn't decided yet if I wanted to take the test. I knew my mom would love it if I did, but I wasn't sure yet what I wanted.

"Polly, what are you reading?" Brooklyn said suddenly, sounding irritated that I hadn't been paying enough attention to her.

I looked up at Brooklyn and realized I couldn't tell the truth, especially since she'd just called the AcaSmackers—members of the Academic Smackdown club—"hopeless überdorks."

"Nothing." I quickly stuffed the letter back into my pocket. "But, hey, there's something super important I need to ask you." I leaned toward Brooklyn and made my eyes go wide, like I was about to ask her the most important question in the history of the world. "What are you wearing to the football game on Friday night?"

At the end of lunch Brooklyn said she'd see us all tomorrow. But the next afternoon in the cafeteria Alyssa refused to sit at the Court.

"No. I'm not eating there again. Not even for you, Kelse. The people over there are lame."

"Will you please lower your voice?" Kelsey said, glancing over her shoulder to make sure no one heard. "And you don't know the people over there, so don't make generalizations. Don't you see? If we join the Court, we could do whatever we wanted and no one could mess with us. It's the only way."

"It's not the only way," Alyssa said. "We don't have to sit there just because you're obsessed with being popular."

"I am *not* obsessed," Kelsey said.

"Can't we go down to the lower level?" Alyssa asked, pointing to the staircase. "I want to check out the choir room before tryouts this afternoon. And I heard a lot of people eat lunch down there."

"You want to eat lunch in the Dungeon?" Kelsey said. "The only rooms down there are the music and drama rooms for all the weird artsy types. The geeks . . . I'm sorry," Kelsey said immediately as Alyssa's face flushed red.

"I may be 'artsy,'" Alyssa said, making air quotes, "but at least I'm not shallow."

Kelsey and Alyssa glared at each other. I stood between them, feeling like a thin paper clip caught between two powerful magnets. Instinctively I grabbed for my heart necklace. It was appropriate that I had the middle section, the one that joined the other two. Because that was always my role—to help Kelsey and Alyssa work things out when they got into one of their famous fights.

Peacemaker Polly, Alyssa always called me.

I twisted my necklace around my finger. Today, I noticed, neither Kelsey nor Alyssa wore theirs. Both of them turned to stare at me. Kelsey's eyes pleading, Alyssa's wary.

"Tell her, Polly," Alyssa said. "Tell her you didn't like sitting there either."

I bit my lip and said nothing. It was true, I hadn't liked sitting at the Court and worrying I might say or do—or be wearing—the wrong thing. Up till then, most of my clothes had come from the thrift shops Alyssa and I shopped at. The previous afternoon I'd begged my mom to take me to the mall. Mom, who had just gotten a big promotion at work, had handed me her credit card and said she'd catch up on paperwork in the food court while I shopped. After I got a haircut, I spent two nerve-racking hours hunting down a week's worth of outfits that I hoped Brooklyn (and Kelsey) would consider Court-worthy. Thankfully, Mom didn't seem to care how much money I'd spent. She even said that since she would be working more hours, I should keep the credit card, just in case.

That morning in homeroom a couple of girls—who'd ignored me the day before—had started asking me all about the Court. When I casually mentioned I'd been invited to eat there again, they said they were having a sleepover that weekend and wanted to know if I could come.

And *that* I liked. A lot. But I knew it wasn't something Alyssa would understand.

Alyssa's eyes hardened. "You can't say it, can you? You can't say what you really think. You've changed your whole look just so those morons over there will think you're cool. Will you change your personality, too? You're plastic, you know that? Plastic Polly—*that's* who you are." Alyssa turned back to Kelsey. "Fine. You two go and sit in Fakeville, but I'm leaving."

Alyssa stomped over to the staircase. After she disappeared down into the Dungeon, Kelsey grabbed my arm and led us to the Court. Once we were settled, Brooklyn asked Kelsey where our friend was.

"She . . . had something she needed to take care of." Kelsey shot me a look that told me to keep quiet.

"Good. I didn't like her attitude," Brooklyn said. "Don't bring her over here tomorrow."

That night I called Alyssa to smooth things over. I didn't want Kelsey to do it, because I was afraid she'd lose her temper and make things worse. I asked Alyssa about the Dungeon, and choir tryouts, and listened while she talked about some new friends she'd made. But it turned out Alyssa felt bad about our fight, and she offered a solution to the lunch problem. "I can't handle being at the Court every day. What if I eat with you guys, like, a couple times a week or something?"

"Um, the thing is, Alyssa," I said, choosing my words carefully, "you have to be invited to the Court."

"And I'm not?"

I didn't know what to say. It occurred to me I could offer to eat with Alyssa in the Dungeon the next day, but I figured if I did, Brooklyn would ban me from the Court too. And that was something I didn't want, I realized. Because even if I didn't really like Brooklyn and some of the other girls at the Court, I *did* like how people were starting to talk to me in class, or in the hallways. I didn't have to even *do* anything; the power of the Court seemed to draw them to me.

Popularity, it seemed to me right then, was the middle school equivalent of a security blanket. Something thick and warm to wrap around yourself to keep you safe from the dangers outside. And incredibly enough, it was being offered to me. (Mostly because I was Kelsey's best friend, but still.) All I had to do was reach out and take it.

And also, I knew if I asked Alyssa not to hang out in the Dungeon, she wouldn't listen. She would tell me if I was really her friend, I wouldn't ask her to give up something so important to her. So why should I give up something *I* wanted, just for her?

"Look, even if we don't hang out at lunch, it doesn't mean anything else has to change."

"Yeah, right," Alyssa said. Then she hung up on me.

I called her back every day for a week, but Alyssa always got her mom to say she was busy or not home or something. Kelsey was furious that Alyssa wouldn't take my calls, and she decided we shouldn't speak to her until Alyssa apologized. Except neither of us had any classes with Alyssa, and her locker was across the school from ours. We rarely saw her—it was like Alyssa didn't exist anymore. But when I began hearing people call me Plastic Polly, I knew who I had to thank.

I threw away my invitation to test for the Star Student program. Who wanted to spend lunchtime being driven over to Maple Oaks High when I had a chance to join the Court? Every day Kelsey and I ate lunch there—until it became clear to everyone that was where we belonged. Sometimes, though, I couldn't help wondering what would have happened if it had been Kelsey who'd stomped away first. Would I have gone to the Court on my own? Or, like Alyssa, would I have sunk into middle school obscurity?

In the waiting room at the hospital, Mrs. Taylor tells me and my mom that Kelsey has a broken wrist, a slight concussion, and a mildly sprained ankle, and she's pretty bruised up—but that Kelsey is really lucky because it could have been so much worse.

"Her room is down the hall, fourth on the left. You girls catch up, and your mom and I will get some coffee from the cafeteria."

Mrs. Taylor takes Molly—Kelsey's little sister—by the hand and heads with Mom to the elevator. After they're gone, I don't immediately go to Kelsey's room. Instead,

I pull my cell phone from my pocket. Maybe it's because I just saw her earlier, but my first instinct is to call Alyssa and let her know Kelsey is okay.

Before I can stop and ask myself why I still have her number in my cell, I'm dialing and the phone is ringing. It's not until Alyssa answers that I realize how stupid I'm being. Although she initially rushed to Kelsey's side, by the time I'd scrambled down the stairs, Alyssa had floated away into the crowd. Maybe she doesn't care how Kelsey is doing.

I'm about to hang up when Alyssa says, "Hello? Polly?"

Stupid caller ID. "Hey, it's me." I explain Kelsey's injuries. Then I say, "But she's okay. They're going to keep her here for a few days before sending her home."

I expect Alyssa to say something snarky, but she doesn't. In fact, she doesn't even seem surprised I called. She just says, "I'm glad."

There's an awkward silence until I say, "I have to—"

"My mom is calling me," Alyssa says.

I think we're both relieved when we hang up.

As soon as I walk into Kelsey's room, I feel nauseous. Colorful bouquets of flowers are spread out on every available surface, making the room smell sickeningly sweet.

"You must have a lot of friends on campus," a nurse is

saying to Kelsey as she makes room on the nightstand for a vase of tulips.

"You have no idea," Kelsey answers, fluffing her hair. "Hey, Polly."

A pile of get-well cards sits next to an arrangement of daisies. Kelsey follows my gaze and says, "Mr. Fish brought them over earlier."

I nod and move over to Kelsey's bed. One card sits next to Kelsey. It's from Melinda and reads:

I know you'll be a great PlanMaster, even if you might be injured! It would really stink if we lost this year. Everyone will be soooo mad if they don't get that concert with Shattered Stars. So get well soon!

I hand the card back to Kelsey and roll my eyes. Typical Melinda.

After the nurse leaves, I sit down on the bed and give Kelsey an awkward hug. "How are you?"

"Okay." Kelsey looks more than okay. A hot-pink cast encloses her left hand, but otherwise she looks great. She's propped up on a pile of pillows, and her sleek black hair is fanned around her like she's a princess. Her face is perfectly made up, and she's wearing her favorite silver hoop earrings.

"I might be out of school for a while," Kelsey says, staring out the window.

I squeeze her good hand. "You'll be back in no time. You look great. Really."

Kelsey shakes her head and looks at me. "My doctor gave me a note. I can be out for three weeks if I want."

"Three weeks? For a broken wrist?"

"*And* a concussion. *And* a sprained ankle," Kelsey says, defensiveness creeping into her voice. "And I hurt everywhere you can imagine."

"Okay. But three weeks? You're not even left-handed. And why would you want to be out of school that long, anyway?"

Kelsey glances at the get-well card from Melinda. "I just—"

"Excuse me, girls." Another nurse walks in, carrying a tray. "Dinner is served. Hospital food at its finest!"

I move off the bed while the nurse places the tray on a table next to Kelsey. I don't get it. Kelsey can be extremely persuasive, which is why Alyssa and I always let Kelsey do the talking whenever the three of us wanted something from one of our parents, so if anyone can talk their doctor into giving them a free pass from school for three weeks, it's Kelsey.

But she never misses school. Not because she loves her classes—Kelsey has an on-again, off-again relationship with her homework—but because as the queen of the Court, Kelsey considers Winston Academy her personal playground. I look around at the bouquets of flowers. It seems to me she'd be dying to go back to school so she could be showered with gifts and attention. So what's going on?

After the nurse leaves, Kelsey takes a bite of chocolate pudding, then makes a face and pushes her tray away. "Since I'm going to be out of school, I called Principal Allen and resigned as the PlanMaster for Groove It Up. I'm really sorry, Polly."

I frown. "What are you apologizing for?"

Kelsey rolls her eyes. "You know, for an A student you can be really slow sometimes. What happens to the vice president when the president is unable to perform his—or her—duties?"

"They—" I stop as the light finally clicks on. "Oh."

"Yep." Kelsey nods and raises her good arm like she's passing a torch. "Congratulations! You are now the new PlanMaster for Winston Academy!"

Chapter 4

✲ ✲ ✲

True Confession: You know how everyone says you shouldn't care what others think about you? Well, I care. A lot.

SOMETIMES I THINK ALYSSA GAVE ME THE WRONG NICKname. Sure, Plastic Polly is clever. But Parrot Polly might have been an even better choice, because my job at the Court—and on the Groove It Up planning committee—is to agree with whatever Kelsey says. It's not like she gets mad at me if I don't. (Not usually, anyway.) But Kelsey always knows what she wants, and most of the time I don't, so it's just easier to go along with her.

Groove It Up is always planned by the members of the Court, with the most popular eighth grader serving as the PlanMaster. It's not a school rule or anything, more like a tradition. And when Mr. Fish holds a meeting for any-one interested in being the PlanMaster, and Queen Kelsey raises her hand and stares down everyone else—silently daring them to cross her—how many other girls are going to volunteer?

Look, it may not be fair. But this is middle school. This is how it *is*.

So the next morning while Mom and I wait outside Principal Allen's office, I'm trying to figure out how to abdicate as the PlanMaster. It has always looked like a ton of work (even though Kelsey didn't seem to be doing a whole lot). And, being the Vice PlanMaster, I get to stand in front of everyone at the Groove It Up pep rallies. But I haven't had to actually *do* anything. It's been nice.

Next to me Mom is firing off texts. Her black pantsuit is freshly pressed, her nutmeg-colored hair is twisted into a severe knot at the nape of her neck, and her ice-blue eyes are narrowed as she taps on her cell. Sometimes I wonder how we could possibly be related when we look so differ-ent. Once, I heard Grandpa Pierce say she was the most striking woman he's ever seen. But no one would ever call me striking. Most things about my appearance—my face, my height, my dirty-blond hair—are average. Except for my eyes. Dad says they're the perfect shade of aqua, like they couldn't decide if they wanted to be green or blue, so they chose somewhere in the middle.

Mom glares at her phone and mutters something under her breath. She's a lawyer for a big firm, but she's not the cool kind of lawyer that struts around in shiny high heels badgering witnesses and demanding that they tell her the truth. More like she spends all day (and many times all night) poring over stacks of boring paperwork in her stuffy office.

Mom says she always knew she wanted to be a lawyer. After she graduated from Harvard, she planned on going to law school. But then she moved back to Maple Oaks in northern California and met Dad. They got married and had me. Mom stayed home with me when I was little, but once I started first grade, she told Dad she was going to law school. I'm probably the only first grader who learned to read by sounding out sentences in legal briefs. Mom just seems happier when she's working and has a huge to-do list. I don't take it personally. Most days, anyway.

"Mom, can I talk to you about something?"

"In a sec," Mom answers, scowling at her phone and texting away.

I wait, but she keeps sending one text after another. Finally I give up and send a text of my own:

I need to talk to you.

"Almost finished. I promise."

"Have you had a chance to look at the application for Camp Colonial?" Mom asks once she's put her phone away.

"That's not what I wanted to talk to you about. And, no, I haven't." A couple of weeks ago Mom handed me an application for this lame camp where you spend half your summer prepping for high school. Look, I may get all As, but that doesn't mean I want to spend every second of my life studying. And sometimes I think Mom looks at my future like it's a geometry problem: What is the shortest distance between point A and point B? With point A being me and point B being Harvard. And the only obstacle standing between Mom's alma mater and her perfect AB line to academic excellence is, well, *me*. That's why I never told her about the invitation I got last year to test for the Star Student program—or the one I received this year either. I knew if she found out, I could kiss any fun I might want to have in middle school good-bye.

"Polly, do you have any idea how many kids would kill for an opportunity like this?"

"I'm guessing somewhere in the range of zero?"

"A little hard work wouldn't hurt, is all I'm saying. Next year you'll be starting high school, and then you'll have to get serious."

"Fine, I will." And then just to annoy her I add, "But in the meantime I'm going to be as unserious as possible. Besides, Kelsey says she wants me to help her train for the high school soccer team over the summer."

"Kelsey says, huh?" Mom frowns. I don't know what her deal is. Lately it seems like she doesn't like Kelsey as much as she used to.

Mom begins to say something else, but she stops when the office door opens and Principal Allen greets us. I expect to hear the stern voice she uses with her students, but instead Principal Allen squeals, "Laura! So good to see you!" and hugs Mom.

"Trudy!" Mom exclaims, all traces of her irritation gone. "It's been ages. How are you? I'll bet when we were cheering for the Winston Wildcats, we didn't think we'd end up here!"

Mom and "Trudy" chatter about the good old days as we walk into the office and settle into chairs around Principal Allen's desk. I can't help feeling a little weird that Mom and Principal Allen know each other. I mean, yeah, I vaguely remember Mom telling me they went to school together, but it's hard to imagine Mom and Principal Allen as middle school cheerleaders.

Next to Principal Allen's desk is a display case holding several trophies. My stomach clenches when I see the three golden microphones—representing Winston's Groove It Up wins over the last three years. A fourth win this year would set a new record. The trophies occupy their own row, but they're not centered. At the end is a large space, like Principal Allen has already reserved the spot for our fourth win.

"Thank you for coming in today," Principal Allen says. "With Kelsey out that means that, as the Vice PlanMaster, Polly is next in line to coordinate Groove It Up. There's much to accomplish in the next few weeks."

Principal Allen looks at me like I'm supposed to speak, to express my gratitude or maybe tell her all about the plans I have for Groove It Up.

"I visited Kelsey in the hospital," I blurt out instead.

Principal Allen nods and waves her hand slightly. "Yes, I've spoken with the Taylors as well, but Kelsey won't be coming back to school until after Groove It Up, and, as they say, the show must go on. The question is, what to do now? There was a school board meeting last night, and questions have arisen regarding Groove It Up and what's best for the school."

"I see," Mom says. I can feel something shift in the atmosphere then, but I can't figure out what.

"Yes," Principal Allen continues, "and we just need a little bit of clarity about what Polly wants to do—if she wishes to continue on as the PlanMaster, or if she wishes to resign." Principal Allen looks at me. "Polly, what are your thoughts?"

My thoughts? The only thought in my head is that I wish I could get away—from Mom, who would sign me up for Harvard right now if she could. And from Principal Allen, who seems more concerned about Groove It Up than she does about Kelsey.

I hesitate before answering, maybe too long, because Principal Allen says, "Polly, there are leftover cookies in the teachers' lounge, just down the hall. Why don't you grab a few—there's milk in the fridge—and we'll pick this up in a few minutes."

I know she's trying to get rid of me—though I'm not sure why—but I don't argue, and try not to run from her office. Inside the teachers' lounge I ignore the cookies and send Kelsey a text:

Are you there?

It takes a minute, but then:

Yes. Hard 2 txt with 1 hand tho.

I'm meeting with Principal Allen. She wants to know if I want to be the PlanMaster or if I want to resign.

I hesitate and then add:

Do you think I could do it?

I had meant to text "should" do it, like whether or not Kelsey thinks it's worth my time. But instead, I typed "could" do it, like I'm wondering if Kelsey thinks I'm able to plan Groove It Up by myself. Which, I guess I am. Wondering, I mean.

I wait for Kelsey to text back.

And wait some more.

When it's clear Kelsey isn't going to respond, I leave the teachers' lounge. The door to Principal Allen's office is cracked open, and I hear whispers. Instinctively, I slow down.

"Oh, Trudy, you mustn't let it get to you," Mom is saying. "People get worked up over Groove It Up. They always have. Remember when we were in eighth grade?"

"Yes, but things are different this year. These prizes

are making everyone crazy. Do you know how many phone calls I've received from parents who want their kid to get a slot on the Talent Team, just so they can get on TV if we win? Or because their kid is dying to see Shattered Stars? Henry Huff is even insisting that this is too important to let the students handle it."

"But Groove It Up is always coordinated by the students. It's tradition."

"That's exactly what I told him, but he's one of our biggest donors, so others listen to him. I need a win here, Laura. Tell me honestly, do you think Polly can get the job done?"

I step closer to the door. I know I should cough, clear my throat, make a bunch of noise, and pretend I haven't just been eavesdropping. But I can't. In the few seconds of silence as we wait for Mom's response, I hear the question a hundred times over:

Can Polly get the job done?

I hear it so many times, it's not until Principal Allen says, "Oh, I see," that I realize Mom never answered the question.

"You have to understand, Trudy," Mom says, sounding embarrassed. "Polly's more of a follower than a leader. And anyway, you know kids today. They're lazy. They're more interested in shopping and texting their friends than working hard."

"So true," Principal Allen says. I don't hear the rest of what she says, because I feel like I've been punched in the gut, and there's a strange buzzing noise in my ears.

The nickname Plastic Polly has always bothered me, but I figured it was mostly just because people were jealous, that they coveted a spot at the Court, and when it was denied, they turned to nastiness as their consolation and decided to dismiss me as shallow and fake. But do people really believe it? Does *my own mother* really believe it?

I feel hollow—like I'm nothing but empty space—as I silently back up a few paces, cough loudly, and clomp through the door. I refuse to look at Mom as I take my seat in front of Principal Allen.

"So, Polly," Principal Allen says, "we were just discussing your options. We feel it's unfair you've been put into this position, that you are now in charge of something as all-consuming as Groove It Up."

Unfair to who? I want to ask, but don't.

"I realize that perhaps you didn't want to be PlanMaster, that it may interfere with your other interests, like . . ." Principal Allen pauses, and frowns.

Like shopping and texting? I say to just myself.

". . . well, whatever they might be," she finishes.

"Yes, Polly," Mom adds. "We want to make sure you have a choice in this. You don't have to be saddled with this responsibility if you don't want to be."

"I can choose what I want to do?" Even my voice sounds hollow. It's funny, but I guess I was expecting Principal Allen to give me a pep talk and tell me I can do it, and go team, and all that junk. And then I'd have to tell her I was choosing to resign. But right now it doesn't feel like much of a choice. It feels like I'm supposed to just go along with Principal Allen so she can give the task to someone else, someone she believes in. This should be easy for me, right? Don't I usually just agree with whatever Kelsey wants when it comes to Groove It Up?

Plastic Polly, Parrot Polly, People Pleaser Polly—they're all me.

My cell pings then, a text from Kelsey:

I'll B helping U the whole time. So of course U can do it!

Suddenly I feel mad. Mad that my own mother won't stick up for me. Mad that she thinks she knows me so well, just because I don't want to go to her stupid pre-high-school camp. Mad that she would criticize me for being on my phone too much, when she practically can't breathe without hers. Mad at myself, that I need Kelsey's advice to make a decision. And mad at Kelsey, too, because her text makes it sound like she thinks I can do it only if she helps me.

"I can choose what I want to do?" I repeat. And this time my voice sounds solid. Not hollow. And definitely not plastic.

"Absolutely. No guilt, and no explanations necessary." I'm staring at Kelsey's text, but I can hear the smile in Principal Allen's voice.

I look up. "Then I choose to do it. I'm going to be the PlanMaster." I stand up and walk out the door, leaving Mom and Principal Allen gaping after me.

Then I text Kelsey:

You've just texted Winston's newest PlanMaster. American River is toast!

Chapter 5

✲ ✲ ✲

True Confession: I know I never would've become popular if I wasn't Kelsey's best friend. I'm pretty sure other people know it too.

THE TEXTS FROM KELSEY START FIVE SECONDS LATER:

The next Groove It Up meeting is 2morrow.

You need 3 judges 4 tryouts.

Do NOT pick Melinda, she'll B impossible 2 work with.

On second thought, Melinda's ruthless. She'll B a great judge.

By the time I've left the administration building, Kelsey has sent five more messages—apparently she texts just fine with one hand. Finally I text her back that I'm going to be late to class. Then I shut off my phone.

Groove It Up fever is spreading around campus. Under a banner I hung up yesterday, a group of soccer players are clowning around and pretending to be members of a boy band. At the drinking fountain a boy is break-dancing while other students clap around him. As I pass the library, I hear several students singing the lyrics to Shattered Stars' newest hit while Mrs. Turner, the school librarian, yells at them to stop being so loud. When I pass Derek's locker, I hear him ask a couple of his friends if they think he'll look good on TV.

Over at the sign-up sheet for tryouts, which I purposely posted across from my locker, students are cheering as Kristy and some other cheerleaders add their names to the list.

"American River is going down!" shouts one boy.

I'm hunting through my locker for my history textbook when I hear Melinda's loud voice behind me. "Guess we have a lot to discuss about Groove It Up."

The cheering stops and a hush falls over the hallway. I hear a couple girls whispering about Kelsey's fall. I turn around. Kristy and everyone else in the hall are watching us.

Melinda is standing in front of me with her arms crossed over her chest. She's wearing lipstick in a disgusting shade of pink that reminds me of raw fish. Lindsey stands beside her, looking nervous as her eyes ping back and forth between Melinda and me.

"Aren't you going to ask me how Kelsey's doing?" I say.

"I don't need to. Everyone already knows Kelsey only broke her wrist and bumped her head."

"Only, right." I stuff a textbook into my backpack. "I'll be sure to tell Kelsey that when I text her. Or when she comes back in a few weeks." For some reason I feel the need to remind Melinda that Kelsey will be back, that the Court won't be without its queen for long.

"Sure, but now that Kelsey's gone, we need to figure out who's the new PlanMaster. Even Kelsey can't do it from a hospital bed."

"*I'm* the new PlanMaster. I just had a meeting with Principal Allen." I decide not to mention that Kelsey voluntarily resigned.

"And she chose you?" I doubt anyone in the crowd hears Melinda's slight emphasis on the word "you," but I can hear it, loud and clear. Melinda sighs and continues,

"Polly, there's a lot more to being the PlanMaster than just wearing cute clothes and telling everyone they're doing a super great job."

I open my mouth, but no sound comes out. Melinda *never* would have said that to me if Kelsey were here.

"Dude, that was *nasty!*" whispers one boy, but he's grinning ear to ear, like he's hoping for a fight.

Everyone is staring at me, and I know they're waiting to see what I'll say. Right now I want to remind Melinda—and everyone else—that in Winston Academy's inner circle there's a pecking order. Which goes: Kelsey, me, and *then* Melinda.

Don't wimp out. Melinda can't get away with that, I say to myself. Then I squinch up my eyes like I'm studying Melinda. "I've got one word for you, Melinda: 'understated.'"

Melinda frowns. "Isn't that two words?"

"No, it's not." I point to my mouth. "If something's fluorescent, it doesn't belong on your face. So unless you want people calling you Sushi Lips, I'd wipe that lipstick off."

Several people in the hall start snickering, and Melinda's face flushes a color that, actually, matches the sushi lipstick.

"And another thing," I say, "now that I'm the Plan-Master, I'm going to need a Vice PlanMaster." I make a show of turning to Lindsey. "Are you up for it? Want to be the Vice PlanMaster?"

Lindsey looks from me to Melinda, then steps closer to me. "Absolutely."

"Great." I turn back to Melinda, and in my best in-command voice I say, "You got a problem with that?"

Melinda glances around at everyone. She starts to say something, but then seems to think better of it. "No," she finally answers.

"Good," I say. "Now go wipe your face."

I'm used to people staring at me. When you're a member of the Court, it goes with the territory. But as word spreads that I'm the new PlanMaster, the looks I get change as I pass from one morning class to another. These stares are questioning, like people are sizing me up.

I decide to skip lunch at the Court. I don't feel like dealing with Melinda. Also, tomorrow afternoon is the next planning meeting, and I have no clue what I'm supposed to do. So far at our meetings we've mostly decorated banners and gossiped. So I head to Mr. Fish's classroom, hoping to get his help.

"Mr. Fish?" I knock on his classroom door, which is open.

"Come in, Miss Pierce." Mr. Fish is leaning back in his chair, reading a magazine.

Besides teaching English, Mr. Fish is Winston's football coach. So today, like every other day, he's wearing shorts and his red Wildcats T-shirt.

"Hey, I wanted to tell you I'm the new PlanMaster for Groove It Up."

Mr. Fish doesn't take his eyes off his magazine. "Yes, I know. I got the memo."

"Okay, so I was just wondering, since there's a meeting tomorrow, what we're doing about Groove It Up?"

"*We* are not doing anything about Groove It Up, but *you*, Miss Pierce, will be doing quite a bit. Prepare yourself for some late nights." Mr. Fish grabs a thick black binder and drops it on his desk with a loud *thunk*. It's labeled THE PLANMASTER'S PLANMASTER. "Here. This will answer any questions you have. I'd suggest you actually read it—something your predecessor has seemed loath to do."

"Okay, but you're the teacher adviser." I pick up the binder; it weighs a ton. "Aren't you supposed to, like, *advise* me?"

"Groove It Up is important to the school and to the Maple Oaks community as a whole—this year in particular. So if you are in desperate need of anything, then, yes, I will assist you. However, the competition is supposed to be a student-led endeavor. Emphasis on 'student.'" Mr. Fish puts down his magazine. "But, Miss Pierce, do you know *why* I'm the teacher adviser to Groove It Up this year?"

"Um, because you have a deep and abiding desire to see Winston Academy beat American River and win cool prizes?"

"Funny. But no. I was out sick the day Principal Allen passed around the sign-up sheet for adjunct duties. Do you know what happens to teachers who are absent on the day Principal Allen decides to do that?"

Before I have a chance to ask him what the word "adjunct" means, he says, "I'll tell you what. They get stuck coordinating eighth-grade graduation in the spring, that's what, as well as coordinating Groove It Up in the fall. Meanwhile, other teachers are wrestling with the strenuous task of deciding which restaurant to hold the staff Thanksgiving dinner at. Do you catch my meaning, Miss Pierce?"

"Are you saying you're not going to help me?"

"I'm saying I could be somewhere else tomorrow afternoon. Attending the Wildcats football practice, for instance. Or I could be home with my wife and my four— count them, *four* daughters—watching a football game."

"Your daughters watch football? With you?" I try, and fail, to keep the skepticism out of my voice.

Mr. Fish picks up his magazine, which I now realize is *Sports Illustrated*. "Yes, Miss Pierce, they do. But I will not be with them. Because I will be here, quietly reading, while you all hold your Groove It Up meeting."

I hug the binder to my chest. My arms are already aching from the weight of it. "So, you're saying I'm on my own here?"

Mr. Fish yawns and flips a page. "Brilliant deduction, Miss Pierce."

After I get home, Mom texts me saying she has to work late and that Dad and I shouldn't wait up for her.

I should probably call Kelsey, but I don't feel like talking to her about the fifteen texts she sent me this afternoon since I shut my phone off. Instead, I open the black binder, prepared to educate myself on all things related to Groove It Up.

Many years ago Groove It Up began as a fun, friendly competition between Winston Academy and American River Middle School. But as the years passed, both schools began to complain of cheating and unfair advantages, so several rules were drafted to guide the competition, resulting in *The PlanMaster's PlanMaster*. It's sort of like a bill of rights, an interschool treaty, and a how-to manual all rolled into one.

Props, costumes, tryout schedules, AV requirements (whatever that means), dress rehearsals—as I turn page after page in the binder, my vision starts to blur. There is *so* much more to being the PlanMaster than I thought. I mean, yeah, on some level I knew it was a lot of work, but I guess when I told Mom and Principal Allen that I wanted the job, I was sort of skipping over the actual, you know, *work* part, and cutting straight to the end, where the PlanMaster of the winning school (namely, me) holds the golden trophy over her head. Now as I flip pages, I'm wondering what I've gotten myself into.

I toss the binder aside, deciding I'll come back to it later tonight. Then I turn on the Food Network and start zoning out to my favorite show—*Chef Sherry*.

I started cooking after Jenna Huff made fun of the muffins I brought to the fifth-grade bake sale. As soon as I plunked them down on the table, she asked, nose wrinkled, where I got them.

"My mom bought them from the grocery store," I said.

"What did you say, Squeaky?" Jenna cocked her ear. After I repeated myself, being sure to deepen my voice,

Jenna said, "You brought store-bought muffins to a bake sale?" She turned around to her little clique and snickered. She didn't even wait until after I left to toss them into the trash. That night I started watching *Chef Sherry*—determined to learn how to bake my own muffins—and discovered I really like to cook. Mom and Dad work late anyway, so now I usually make dinner for everyone. I don't mind, and I know Dad is glad someone actually uses the kitchen they just remodeled.

After *Chef Sherry* is over, I decide to make spaghetti. Sometimes when I'm cooking pasta for myself I just boil the noodles and pour soy sauce over them. I call it soy sauce spaghetti.

Tonight, though, I chop up onions and mushrooms and sauté them in butter and garlic. A few more minutes and I've added in ripe tomatoes, black olives, and fresh basil and oregano. Then I boil water for spaghetti and grate parmesan cheese. Once everything's done, I dish up a plate for me and Dad and light the candles in our dining room. And then I wait.

When the candles are burning low, I call Dad's cell.

"Dad?"

"Polly, how's my girl?" Dad's voice sounds tired, and in the background I hear a scratching noise.

I imagine him in his office—kind eyes, graying hair, suit rumpled. He's the executive director of a group home for foster kids, so he deals with some crazy situations. Dad is pretty laid-back and feels like as long as I'm getting good grades and staying out of trouble, everything's fine.

"Are you still at work? I made you dinner."

"Oh, Polly, I'm so sorry . . ."

Dad breaks off, and in the silence that follows I hear the scratching noise again. Only now I realize it's not scratching at all. It's the sound of someone crying. A girl, I think. I imagine she's in Dad's office. Maybe she's just received bad news. Maybe she thought she'd get to go home with a foster family today, and can't. And maybe my dad is the only one she can talk to about it.

"Polly," Dad says, "I really am sorry. I'll finish right up and—"

"You know what, Dad? It's cool. Really. I'll just leave some in the fridge for you."

After I hang up the phone, I turn the TV back on and flip channels until I come to a football game. I imagine Mr. Fish watching the game with his wife and four daughters. Then I look around at my empty house, and the plate of cold spaghetti sitting on the dining room table. Right now football doesn't seem like such a bad thing.

Chapter 6

☆ ☆ ☆

True Confession: Being popular feels like I'm always walking on a tightrope. One false move, and it's a long, long way down.

I MAY BE THE ONLY EIGHTH GRADER WHO REGULARLY gives herself pep talks. I guess some people try to psych themselves up before a test or something, but that's not what I'm talking about. I mean I stand in front of a mirror—whether it's the one on my closet door, in a bathroom, or the mirror I stuck on the inside of my locker door—and talk to myself. (When I do this at school, I whisper so no one hears.) And I say things like:

You are confident.

You are in control.

You. Are. Awesome.

And if you act like you think you're awesome, other people will think so too.

I got the idea to do this when Mom was listening to a podcast of her favorite motivational speaker. Hey, it might sound lame, but believe me, to survive life at the Court, you need all the pep talks you can get. Being popular looks like a lot of fun—and I'm not going to lie, sometimes it really is—but sometimes it's stressful, too.

After school ended, I dashed over to Chip's and picked up some cheesecakes for the planning committee meeting. Now I'm standing in front of my locker mirror hoping no one hears me talk to myself.

"You've got this meeting in the bag. It'll be no problem. You—"

"Hey, Pretty Polly!"

I jump and turn around. Derek Tanner is standing behind me, dressed in his football uniform. His hair is slicked into a crown of spikes. Even with the gallon of hair gel he must've used, he still smells like cardboard.

"Oh, hey, Derek. What's up?"

Derek holds up his helmet. "On my way to practice. What about you?"

"I'm going to the planning committee meeting. I was just . . . I just got back from picking up snacks." I gesture to the bags from Chip's on the floor.

Derek picks up the bag with the cheesecakes, but leaves the bag of paper plates and forks. "Want me to carry this for you?"

"Um . . . sure. That would be super great." I grab the other bag, and we start down the hall.

We walk in silence for a minute, and it occurs to me maybe I've been too hard on Derek. Maybe he's been hanging around because he really likes me, not just because he wants a slot on the Talent Team.

"You're in Mr. Fish's English class, right?" I ask. "We have book reports due in a couple weeks. What are you doing yours on?"

"Um . . ." Derek thinks for a minute. A long minute. Finally he shrugs. "I guess I haven't thought about it yet. What about you?"

After I tell him the title of my book, he says, "*Little Women*? What, are they midgets or something?"

"No, Derek. And you're supposed to say 'little people,' not 'midgets.' It's rude."

We arrive outside of Mr. Fish's classroom, and Derek hands me the bag. Then he leans forward, and I get a big blast of pickle breath. "I can't wait for tryouts. I have a great surprise in store for you. I think you'll really like it."

Before I can answer, I hear Melinda shout, "Polly! You're late!"

Derek pokes his head into the classroom. "Hey, Coach!" he says to Mr. Fish, who, true to his word, is sitting at his desk flipping through *Sports Illustrated*. "We'll miss you at practice today."

Mr. Fish grumbles that Derek and the rest of the team had better not take it easy just because he's not there.

"Wouldn't dream of it, Coach," Derek says. Then he turns back to me and waves. "Catch you later."

"You're late," Melinda repeats as I struggle through the door into the classroom.

"I was picking up cheesecakes from Chip's." Looking around, I see that Kristy, Lindsey, and a couple other seventh graders we allowed on the committee are already here. They've pushed their desks into a small circle.

"That's nice," Melinda says. "Maybe we should just call you the SnackMaster, too."

"Or maybe not," I say. Both of us are singsonging our words, but from the way Lindsey and everyone else is looking at us, I can tell they feel the tension between Melinda and me. I heard a couple people call Melinda "Sushi Lips" in the hallway today. And she barely spoke to me at lunch.

Just then there's a knock at the door. "Is this the Groove It Up meeting?"

I turn around. Standing behind me is Jenna Huff.

Jenna Huff has fluffy brown hair—that has always reminded me of a stuck-up poodle—and a small ski jump nose, which is currently turned upward as she stares at me.

"What are *you* doing here?" I ask rudely before I can help myself.

"I invited her," Melinda says. "We need another person now that Kelsey's out."

Jenna looks at Melinda. "You didn't tell me Plast—" She stops, and then says, "You didn't tell me *Polly* was the PlanMaster." There's disgust in Jenna's voice, and she turns slightly toward the door. As if the fact that I'm the Plan-Master changes everything and Jenna may just walk away.

Which would be A-okay with me. And besides, by now everyone in school knows I'm the PlanMaster, so I think Jenna's just saying it to be mean.

"Principal Allen made Polly the PlanMaster." Melinda's voice sounds sour.

"All right." Jenna gives a gigantic sigh, like she's doing everyone a great big favor, and sits down at an empty desk.

Okay, here's another reason why I don't like Jenna

Huff: When we were in fifth grade, she wanted to do a mother-daughter book club. I thought it was a great idea, even though Kelsey, Alyssa, and I never hung out with Jenna and her friends. When I told Jenna I wanted to join, but that sometimes my mom couldn't make it because she was working, Jenna just smirked and said, "Duh. You have to have a mother to go to a mother-daughter book club."

Jenna smirks at me now as I pass out plates of cheese-cake to the committee. Out of the corner of my eye I see Melinda glance at Jenna, then at me, and then roll her eyes. There's something about her look, like she sought Jenna out and discovered who I was before I became a member of the Court. The bookworm with the squeaky voice.

"Here." I hold a plate out to Mr. Fish.

He looks over the top of his magazine. "Is that pumpkin cheesecake?" I nod, and he takes the plate. "Pumpkin cheesecake is my favorite," he says, almost grudgingly.

I tell everyone we'll start after we've eaten, and I take my time while I read through the speech I wrote last night. The truth is I've never led a meeting before. It's not that I haven't ever been on a school committee. I was on the deco-rating committee for the back-to-school dance we had last month, but I mostly just took notes and ran errands while Kelsey led the meetings.

I'm stalling for another reason too. Last night I meant to read *The PlanMaster's PlanMaster*, but it took me a while to write the speech. Then I had to pick out my outfit for today, something that usually takes me about an hour. After that I had a ton of homework to do. So, yeah, it didn't happen.

But I figure today I'll give my speech, call it a day, and we'll just get more done at the next meeting. When everyone has finished eating, I take out a notebook and a pen and call for everyone's attention. "Look, Jenna," I say, "we don't have a lot of time, but before we start I want to catch you up about the planning committee—"

"Both of my older sisters were PlanMasters for Groove It Up," Jenna interrupts. "So I already know what the planning committee does—probably more than you do."

"Fine. Have it your way," I say through gritted teeth.

I'm about to launch into my speech when Kristy says, "I have a question. How come every time my girls and I want to practice our routine in the auditorium, the drama club is using it?"

"Um," I begin, "I'm not—"

"That's probably because Polly never booked the auditorium," Jenna interrupts again. Then she turns to me. "You need to talk to Mrs. Marsden, the drama teacher, and book the auditorium and the practice rooms so people can rehearse for Groove It Up."

"Okay, I can do that." I decide not to mention that Kelsey probably should've done that last week. "But anyway, I wanted to say—"

"I have a question too," says Naomi Stillwell, a seventh grader. "We only need three judges for tryouts on Friday. So do we all have to be there? Because—"

"Yes," Jenna answers. "Everyone needs to be there. The rest of the committee needs to keep the peace in the auditorium while the judges watch auditions in the practice room. Polly can order pizza for us." Jenna turns to me. "You need to order pizza. It'll be a long night, trust me."

"Good point," Melinda says, and flashes me an evil grin. "It's nice to have someone around here who actually knows what they're doing."

"Oh, Jenna," Lindsey says, "what about . . ."

I tune out while Jenna answers people's questions and look down at the speech I wrote. I was going to give the girls a pep talk, and tell them we needed to pull together, that Kelsey's injury was a big blow to the committee, and that we had a long road ahead of us, but if we worked together as a team, I was confident we could win Groove It Up.

Okay, I admit it. I copied my speech from my favorite

movie lines. But still, it's a good speech. And with Jenna coming in and taking over, it looks like I won't be able to give it.

I glance over and see Melinda grinning at me. "I have some things I need to say," I whisper to her.

"I've got one word for you," Melinda whispers back. "Sushi Lips."

"That's two words, Melinda."

Melinda shrugs like she couldn't care less. "Whatever. Don't pout to me just because Kelsey isn't here and you two can't gang up on everyone else."

I look at the clock above Mr. Fish's desk. The meeting is almost over, and I haven't said one thing. So much for being a good PlanMaster. I smile halfheartedly at Mr. Fish, who has finished his cheesecake and is staring at me.

Mr. Fish clears his throat, interrupting Jenna, who's going into great detail about the outfits she thinks we should wear to Groove It Up. "If I recall correctly, Miss Taylor already ordered T-shirts for the planning committee." Mr. Fish glances at me. "In fact, Zack called and said you can pick them up at the mall anytime."

Zack Wilson, owner of Zack's Shirt Shack, is a big supporter of Groove It Up. This year he was selected to be our emcee.

"I can do that tonight," I say quickly.

"Fine." Jenna looks irritated. "Then after that we need to— Polly . . ." She pauses and taps on my notebook. "Shouldn't you be taking notes on all this?"

I pick up my pen and start to write, but then quickly put it down. "You know what, Jenna? We do need someone to take notes." I toss my notebook and pen at her. "And as the PlanMaster, I'm selecting *you* to be our secretary."

Jenna starts to protest, but I cut her off, "Unless you've decided you don't want to be a part of the committee?"

Jenna grudgingly flips open the notebook. If I looked closely enough, I bet I could actually see steam coming out of her ears.

Mr. Fish clears his throat again. He has resumed reading his magazine. "You girls should also know that the coin toss meeting with American River's planning committee is tomorrow afternoon. I need at least one of you to attend with me."

"Okay," Jenna says quickly. "Melinda and I will go. Kristy should come too."

"Since I'm the PlanMaster," I say with a look at Jenna, "I think I'll go too." Before Jenna can speak, I turn toward the rest of the committee and add, "And we also need to talk about tryouts. We need three judges."

"Done," Melinda says.

I pause and look at Melinda. "What do you mean, 'done'?"

Melinda shrugs. "Jenna and I decided we'd be the judges."

"Oh yeah?" I say. "How do you figure the two of you will be judges?"

"Simple. Kristy can't be a judge if she's trying out. And Lindsey and everyone else are seventh graders, so they can't be judges. So that leaves me and Jenna."

"Wow," I say, crossing my arms. "Sounds like you've got it all figured out. So, then, who's the third judge?"

Melinda looks at me like I'm a total idiot. "You are. You're the PlanMaster, aren't you?"

Chapter 7

✩　✩　✩

True Confession: If my parents ever let me get a dog,
I'd name her Roosevelt, after Eleanor Roosevelt.
But I'd just call her Rosie for short.

AM I THE PLANMASTER? BECAUSE IT DIDN'T FEEL LIKE it at the meeting. It felt like I was stuck in my usual role, except this time instead of agreeing with everything Kelsey said, I was supposed to agree with whatever Jenna and Melinda said. After we established that, yes, I was the third judge, I brought the meeting to a close, saying I needed to be somewhere. Really, I just wanted to get out of there as quickly as possible.

On the ride over to the mall, Mom fires question after question at me about the meeting, even though I tell her three times I don't want to talk about it. Once we arrive, she heads to the food court while I hurry to Zack's Shirt Shack to pick up the Groove It Up T-shirts.

Inside, Zack shows me the shirts Kelsey ordered. They're pink and glittery with the word "Staff" written in swirly purple writing. When I go to pay for them, Zack shakes his head, and his brown corkscrew curls bounce in all directions.

"It's on the house this year, since you guys made me emcee."

I thank Zack and leave. Standing outside the shop is a boy about my age holding a note card in one hand and a leash in the other. A white toy poodle dressed in a plaid sweater is at the other end of the leash, his tail wagging furiously.

"Ooooh, what a cute dog!" I crouch down to pet him, and am immediately rewarded with several humid licks on my face. I nuzzle him back. "I've always wanted a dog." Actually, I've always wanted any kind of pet, but Mom is allergic to most animals, so that was never an option.

"You want this one?" the boy asks. "Cuz you're welcome to him."

The dog jumps up onto my lap, barking and licking my face.

"Percy, down!" The boy tugs on the leash. "I mean it. Get down! I'm so sorry."

"No problem. His name's Percy?"

"Actually, his name's Pretty Percy—please don't make me tell you why. I'm Justin."

"I'm Polly." I stand up and realize that Justin is *tall*. Like, basketball player tall. He's wearing silver wire-framed glasses over eyes the color of green apples. He has a chipped front tooth, which makes his smile seem crooked. I take a step backward because—thanks to Pretty Percy—I probably now smell like dog breath.

"How—" I stop, because my voice sounds squeaky.

You are a member of the Court, I tell myself sternly. *You can talk to a boy without turning into a complete moron.*

"How long have you had Pretty Percy?" I ask, and this time my voice sounds confident.

"He's my grandma's, actually. We're shopping for a present for my mom." Justin gestures to an antiques shop. "They don't want poodles in their store, and I have something for school I have to pick up from Zack's anyway." He waves the note card in his hand. "So I'm studying for something until Gran finishes up. You don't happen to remember who ruled England from 1558 to 1603, do you?"

"Queen Elizabeth the First," I say automatically.

Justin whistles. "Wow."

"What do you mean by that?" I place my hand on my

hip and study Justin, to see if he looks surprised, like he can't believe someone like me would know the answer to a question like that. But then I realize Justin doesn't know I'm popular. He definitely doesn't go to Winston. I would remember a boy like Justin.

Here's the thing: Sometimes it feels like people expect me to be a total airhead because I'm popular. I mean, I know I don't talk about my grades a lot, but last year in an assembly when Principal Allen called my name for honor roll, I heard Bethany Perkins—the editor of the school newspaper—whisper to her friend, "Plastic Polly made the honor roll? Seriously?" I wanted to lean over and tell Bethany that not only had I made honor roll, but I also knew the answer to the question she'd missed at the last Academic Smackdown meet. (Kelsey had to go to the meet because she needed to earn extra credit, and I tagged along.) I didn't say anything, though, because I was sitting with a bunch of girls from the Court.

"I just mean, wow, that's impressive," Justin says, and he sounds like he means it.

We stand there awkwardly while Pretty Percy sniffs my sandals. "If you want, I could watch Pretty Percy while you're in Zack's." I'm not particularly in a hurry to get back to Mom so she can finish grilling me about the Groove It Up meeting.

And, you know, the fact that Justin is cute—in a brainy sort of way—doesn't hurt either.

Justin cocks his head. "You're not, like, some kind of dognapper are you? I'm kidding!" he adds when I start to protest. He hands me Pretty Percy's leash.

While I wait, I pet Pretty Percy and check my cell phone. I missed five texts from Kelsey, all of them demanding to know how the meeting went.

"Okay, all finished," Justin says, stepping out of the shop. He's carrying a large bag. He clears his throat, and his Adam's apple bobs up and down. "Hey, I was wondering if—"

Just then an elderly lady comes up behind Justin and says, "Ready to go?"

Justin glances at his grandma, then back at me. "Um . . . nice meeting you," he mutters finally.

I'm hoping he'll finish what he was about to say, but when he doesn't, I hand him Pretty Percy's leash. "Nice meeting you, too."

And I can't quite keep the disappointment out of my voice.

"What do the shirts look like?" Mom asks when I plop down across from her. She's already halfway through her slice of pizza.

I open my bag from Zack's and hold up a T-shirt.

"It's pretty. Your dinner is getting cold." Mom pushes a slice of pepperoni pizza toward me.

"Yeah, Zack's was . . . busy." I start picking off the pepperoni slices. I actually can't stand meat on my pizza, but I love the taste of pepperoni grease on cheese.

"Hmm," Moms says, and I can tell she's not really listening. She opens her purse and takes out the application for Camp Colonial. "Guess what I found in the garbage this morning?"

"Mom," I groan, "I don't want to talk about this right now." I make a mental note that next time I'll tear the application into shreds before I toss it into the trash. Then I take a large bite of pizza, and make a show of chewing, hoping she'll drop it.

Fat chance. "Well, when *do* you think you'll find the time to talk about it?" Mom asks. "This is a very prestigious camp, and spots are limited. And I don't see what the problem is. I thought you wanted to visit Boston."

"Boston?" I swallow and look up. I do want to go to Boston. Every time we study American history in school, I think it would be cool to see all the old historical buildings.

Mom frowns. "Polly, did you even *read* the application?"

"I've been busy—and now with being PlanMaster for Groove It Up—"

"I understand that Groove It Up is time-consuming, but you still need to focus on your future."

"I know, but Groove It Up is important," I say, thinking fast. "I bet it would look great on a college application." Bingo, the two words that usually get Mom's attention (and get her off my back), especially when I say them together. College! Application!

Except it doesn't seem to have the same effect this time. "Is that why you're doing this?" Mom leans forward. "Or is this about having fun with your friends from the Court?"

Why *am* I doing this? To prove I'm not Plastic Polly? To prove I can be a leader? Because if so, I blew it royally at the meeting. "So what if it is?" I push my plate away, because I don't feel hungry anymore. "What's wrong with doing something just because it's fun? Not everything has to be about work." I tap the application.

"*Are* you having fun? Because I tried to talk to you about the meeting, and you refused to discuss it."

"Because it was horrible, okay? Melinda invited Jenna Huff to be on the committee, and the two of them basically shut me out of the meeting. *That's* how it went. There. Are you happy now?"

"Jenna Huff?" There's an edge to Mom's voice. It's slight, but it's there. Mom likes Mrs. Huff about as much as I like Jenna. When we were in Winston's elementary section, Mrs. Huff was president of the PTA. Once, she sent home a note saying it would be nice if the parents who didn't regularly volunteer gave the other mothers a break, and would Mom mind handling the decorations for the class Christmas party?

Mom, possessed with more determination than I saw when she studied for the bar exam, decided she'd show prissy Mrs. Huff she could make decorations just like any other mother.

Mom stayed up all night snipping snowflakes, frosting gingerbread houses, stringing popcorn for the class Christmas tree, and making ornaments. (She had glitter stuck in her hair for days afterward.) When she brought her box of decorations to school, Mrs. Huff took it by the tips of her fingers, as though Mom's creations might soil her. "Laura, dear," she said, "these are quite, um, *cute*. But usually we just buy the decorations."

After that, Mom threw away anything the PTA ever sent her.

Mom's cell phone rings. She checks it and says, "Polly, I'm so sorry, but I have to take this. Hello? Hello? Are you there? Yes, just a minute." Mom covers the receiver with her hand. "The reception here is bad. I'm going to step away for a sec."

"Fine," I call as she walks away. "Nice talking to you."

My cell pings then. It's another text from Kelsey:

Melinda just texted. She has serious issues with how you handled the meeting. Call me!!

How *I* handled the meeting? Is she serious? I drop my phone onto the table, harder than I intended, so it makes a clattering sound.

"Everything okay?" says a voice behind me.

I turn. Justin is holding a plate with a slice of pepperoni pizza. He smiles tentatively. "Can I sit down?"

"Sure." I can feel my heart quickening, and I sit up a little straighter. "Where are your grandma and Pretty Percy?"

Justin makes a face. "Percy got pizza sauce on his sweater. So now they're over at the pet shop, getting him a new one."

"Oh, that's a good idea." I try not to laugh, and fail. Justin laughs too.

"How come you're abusing your phone?" Justin asks.

I look away and shrug. "It's just been a bad day." I glance

back at Justin and add, "I mean, it hasn't been all bad. I mean . . ." Then I stop talking, because I can feel my face flushing redder than the glob of pizza sauce on Justin's plate.

My cell phone pings once. Then twice. Then again. Three more texts from Kelsey:

You haven't called me. Call me!!

Melinda says you need major help being the PlanMaster.

Are you ignoring me?

"Are you sure you're okay?" Justin asks. "You look kind of stressed."

"I guess I am." I push my phone away as it pings yet again. "There's this project at school I'm in charge of, and sometimes I think anyone else in the world would be better at it, you know?"

Justin smiles. "I know the feeling. What project is it?"

"I'm the PlanMaster at my school for something called Groove It Up, and it's *not* going well."

Justin gets a strange look on his face. "Oh, look, Polly, I think—"

"The thing is," I say, "my best friend, who was supposed to be the PlanMaster, sort of dropped out, so now I'm in charge. But no one seems to think I can pull it off."

Justin tries to say something, but I cut him off, because it feels good to talk to someone, even if it's a (cute!) boy I don't know. "Also, there are girls on my planning committee who are trying to take over, and I don't know how to deal with it." I tell Justin a few more things, like how Mr. Fish refuses to help me, and how Kelsey planned to give half the slots to our cheerleading team. I also tell him how Melinda always says if our school wins, then the Plan-Master deserves the credit, but how I think she also means if Winston loses, then the PlanMaster is to blame. And I wonder if I could get banished from the Court.

Because that can happen. Last year Haley Miller made the mistake of saying yes when Gavin Clark asked her to the Spring Fling dance. Apparently, he'd been Brooklyn Jones's secret crush forever. One day Haley was popular. The next she was banished from the Court. Frozen out. She finished the rest of the year in exile, eating lunch by herself in the library. Because once Brooklyn made it clear Haley wasn't her friend, no one else wanted to be Haley's friend either.

I'm wondering now if I should have thought of that before deciding to become the PlanMaster. I'm starting to feel stupid for not resigning when I had the chance.

No guilt, and no explanations necessary, Principal Allen had said. But if I resign now, won't that just prove what she and Mom thought? That I'm too frivolous, too plastic to do anything other than hang at the Court and text?

When I finish, Justin, who looks really uncomfortable, says, "Um, Polly, I think I should tell you—"

"I'm so sorry," Mom says, walking up behind Justin. "That took longer than I expected. We need to get going. I have to go back to the office." Mom looks stressed. She barely glances at Justin before turning around and heading for the exit.

"Okay." I grab my phone and read the last text from Kelsey—she's threatening to break out of the hospital, hunt me down, and pummel me with her cast if I don't call her back ASAP.

"Thanks for listening," I say to Justin, feeling shy all of a sudden. "I'll see you around." I run to catch up to Mom.

"I'm sure you will," he calls behind me.

And I don't know why, but this time Justin's the one who sounds disappointed.

Chapter 8

✡ ✡ ✡

True Confession: I practice different "looks" in front of
the mirror. A useful one is my Popular Polly look,
a mixture of indifference and boredom. I use it when I
think someone has said something mean about me.

THE GROOVE IT UP ANNUAL COIN TOSS TRADITIONALLY
happens about two weeks before the actual event. The planning committees for both schools meet and toss a coin to
determine which campus will host Groove It Up. It's con-
sidered home court advantage. Last year American River
won the toss. The year before that as well. They have a habit
of winning the coin toss but losing Groove It Up.

This year the meeting is in Mr. Fish's classroom. I
arrived five minutes early and helped him line up desks
in two rows facing each other. Winston's entire planning committee decided to come, and we're sitting on

the side facing the door, waiting for American River's committee to show up. They're late, and people are getting antsy.

While we wait, I'm reading a text from Kelsey. She came home from the hospital this morning and wants me to walk over to her house after the meeting is over. Next to me, Lindsey is filing her nails. On my other side Melinda is hunched over a fashion magazine with Jenna, taking some kind of quiz. Surprisingly, Mr. Fish isn't wearing his shorts and Wildcats T-shirt. He's wearing jeans, a white shirt, and a tie. The rest of the committee sits on his other side, chatting.

"When are they coming?" Kristy fidgets in her cheer uniform. "I'm going to be late to practi—"

Kristy breaks off at the sound of several feet stomping up the hallway, like a small marching band is coming our way. Then there's a loud knock at the door.

"Everyone ready?" Mr. Fish asks. After we nod he says, "Come in!"

The door opens, and a man who I assume is American River's teacher adviser strides in wearing a black polo shirt and khaki pants. He holds a clipboard in one hand.

Several students file in after him. They halt and take their seats, all at the same time, like they're doing some kind of military exercise. Each of them is also wearing a polo shirt and khakis. They all hold clipboards. And none of them smile.

"Good afternoon," Mr. Fish says when they're all seated. "Welcome to Winston Academy. Let's go around and introduce ourselves."

Mr. Fish lets American River go first. The teacher adviser introduces himself as Mr. Pritchard, and then the students introduce themselves. I'm not really paying attention, because I'm texting Kelsey back under my desk. Until I hear a boy say, "I'm Justin Goodwin. I'm the PlanMaster for American River."

I freeze in midtext. I know that voice. I just heard it last night. From Justin at the mall. The Justin who didn't want to tell me how Pretty Percy got his name. The Justin I spilled my guts to about Groove It Up.

Justin is American River's PlanMaster? I look up. Justin is sitting directly across from me. He's staring at me with wide eyes and a pale face. He shakes his head slightly and mouths something at me. *I'm sorry,* maybe?

"Say 'Polly,'" Melinda spits, jabbing me in the side with her elbow, way harder than she needs to. "It's your turn. Stop being such a spaz."

"Uh, Polly Pierce." Then I give Justin my best Popular

Polly look and add, "I'm the PlanMaster for Winston Academy."

Mr. Fish launches into a speech about how much he's looking forward to partnering with American River and how he hopes we can all work together to make it a great event for both our schools and for Maple Oaks as a whole. I'm surprised, because it sounds like he actually cares. I tune out after a while, though, because I'm thinking back to last night. Did I tell Justin anything really important? I feel like the biggest idiot on the face of the planet. Of all the people I could've confided in, it had to be American River's PlanMaster?

Justin could've said something like, "Hey, I'm your rival, so you might want to shut it." But did he do that? No. He just sat there acting like he cared. He was probably only listening so he could spy on me.

"Before we get to the coin toss," Mr. Pritchard says, "I'd like to direct everyone's attention to one of the rules." He opens a copy of *The PlanMaster's PlanMaster* and reads, "A school club or organization may only participate in one act in the talent competition. Similarly, a student may not participate in more than one act for each annual competition." Mr. Pritchard stops reading and looks pointedly at Kristy. "This would include the cheerleading squad."

I look over at Justin, who is steadfastly staring at his shoes. He *was* spying on me!

"Thank you for sharing that," Mr. Fish says, seeming a little puzzled. "That's very helpful."

While Mr. Fish makes a couple more announcements, a white-faced Melinda, who seems to have forgotten she's not speaking to me, whispers, "How did they know?"

"I have no idea," I whisper back. I glare at the American River team and try to look properly outraged.

Melinda writes something in the margin of her magazine and pushes it over to me:

I TOLD Kelsey not to have so many
seventh graders on the committee.
They can't Keep their mouths shut.

Totally, I write back.

Melinda glances at the seventh graders next to Mr. Fish, a look of disgust on her face, then turns back to me and rolls her eyes. I roll mine back. For the moment it looks like all's forgiven between us. I feel bad throwing the seventh graders under the bus, but what can I do, tell Melinda that last night I was blabbing our strategy to American River's PlanMaster? Forget being banished from the Court. I might get banished from Winston Academy altogether.

"All right." Mr. Pritchard pulls a penny from his pocket. "I'll just toss the coin. We call heads."

"Wait a minute," Mr. Fish says. "That's not a regulation coin toss."

"Excuse me?" Mr. Pritchard frowns.

"I think we should observe certain rules, just as they do in football."

"Football?" Mr. Pritchard says contemptuously.

"Yes," Mr. Fish answers. His voice sounds pleasant, but his eyes harden as he adds, "It's amazing to me how American River seems to win the coin toss year after year. What do you think are the odds of that?"

Then Mr. Fish directs everyone to stand in a circle at the side of the room. Justin slides into place next to me and starts to whisper, "Polly, I really—" but I move over in between Melinda and Lindsey before he can finish.

"Are you satisfied?" Mr. Pritchard says to Mr. Fish, who nods. "All right, then. Let's get this over with. We call heads."

"Hold it," Mr. Fish says. "Show me the coin."

"Why?" Mr. Pritchard asks.

"Because I want to make sure it isn't a two-headed coin."

Mr. Pritchard sputters and turns red, but while he's defending his integrity and talking about the importance of trust between rivals, I notice he slips his penny into his pocket. And maybe it's just me, but does the coin he's holding now look just a little bit shinier?

While Mr. Fish examines the coin, I close my eyes, because I can see Justin is trying to get my attention. If Melinda or anyone else finds out I was hanging out with him last night, I am so dead.

Once Mr. Fish is satisfied the penny is genuine, Mr. Pritchard calls heads again and tosses it into the air. A glint of copper catches the sunlight streaming in from the window. When the penny hits the floor, it bounces and rolls in between Kristy's and Jenna's shoes until it spins and lands under a desk.

"Nobody move," Mr. Pritchard says. "I'll check the coin."

"I'll check it with you," Mr. Fish says. Before Mr. Pritchard can move, Mr. Fish has turned aside the desk so they can both stare at it.

"It's tails!" Mr. Fish hollers.

"Are you sure it's tails, because it looks like it could be—"

"It's tails," Mr. Fish says. "Tails, definitely."

Once we're seated again, Mr. Fish says, "We're happy

to host Groove It Up. I think you'll find that Winston's auditorium is quite sizeable and can easily accommodate both schools."

Mr. Pritchard smiles, although it looks like the effort might kill him. And I'm pretty sure I hear him mutter something about "snobby private school kids" before he says, "Thank you."

A girl from American River—Montana, I think—who has beady black eyes, slicked-back brown hair, and really chubby cheeks says, "We have a list of things we'll need from you as the host school." She looks expectantly at Justin, who's staring at the fire alarm, looking like he wishes someone would give it a good pull. Then, with a disgusted grunt, she picks up Justin's clipboard and says, "Each act from our Talent Team has a list of needs."

"You had tryouts already?" I ask.

"We had them last month. Our students have been perfecting their acts for the last several weeks. You'd better prepare yourself." Montana regards our team coolly. "We're through accepting second place. The concert and the spot on *Good Morning, Maple Oaks* are ours."

"Oh yeah?" Melinda says. "Well, that's just too bad, because our school has quite a nice collection of trophies. And we'd like another one." She wrinkles her nose at

Montana like she smells something rotten. "Those are nice cheeks you have there. Shouldn't you be somewhere else right now, storing up nuts for the winter?"

Mr. Fish tells Melinda she's out of line, but no one listens to him. Montana's cheeks swell even larger, and she says something equally nasty to Melinda, which is followed by a cutting remark from Jenna. Then both teams are standing up and yelling, except for me. And for Justin, who's leaning forward trying to get my attention.

"All right, that's enough!" Mr. Fish hollers. "This meeting is now over!"

I ignore Justin and leave the classroom, barely hearing Melinda's and Montana's voices as they continue trading insults. I pull out my phone and send Kelsey a text.

I'm on my way. I NEED to talk to you. Right now!

Fifteen minutes later I'm standing in front of Kelsey—who's lying on her bed, propped up on a sea of hot-pink throw pillows—feeling like a chastened general giving a bad report to her queen.

"Let me get this straight," Kelsey says, settling back under her red quilt. "Justin, the guy you were going on and on about last night, is American River's PlanMaster?"

I nod, and blink several times. Every time I walk into Kelsey's room, I feel like I need sunglasses. Last year she decided to decorate her room in bright shades of red and hot pink, saying they were her power colors. I've never told her this, but personally I think it looks like a valentine upchucked all over the place.

"It gets worse." I tell her all about the meeting and how her brilliant plan to feature the cheerleading squad has been crushed.

When I've finished, Kelsey throws a pillow at me, which I catch. "That's just great, Polly. The next time you decide to blab your business to a random guy at the mall, do me a favor? Make sure he's not your competition."

"Did you know?" I toss the pillow back at Kelsey, which she catches.

"Did I know what?"

"That giving the cheerleaders multiple slots in the show was against the rules?"

Kelsey shrugs. "Have you seen how thick that Plan-Master guide thingy is?"

Which is basically her way of saying no.

My cell rings—it's a number I don't recognize—and I answer it.

"Polly? Don't hang up. It's Justin."

"Justin?" I look at Kelsey and mouth, *It's him!* I punch the speakerphone button so she can hear.

Kelsey hurls the pillow at me. I duck, and it sails into a bunch of get-well cards on her desk. "You tell that lying, spying little—"

I motion for her to be quiet. To Justin I say, "That was my friend. Don't mind her. What do you want? And how did you get this number, anyway?"

"It's on the list of contact numbers Mr. Fish passed out after you left. You ran out of there really fast, and I wanted to talk to you."

"Why? So you could spy on me some more? Did you tell your whole team about me?"

"Hang up!" Kelsey yells. "He's probably spying on you right now!" Kelsey throws another pillow at me, and it hits me in the head.

"Don't hang up!" Justin sounds panicky. "I'm not spying on you, and I wasn't last night either. I tried to tell you not to talk about Groove It Up, but—"

"Tried!" Kelsey shouts. "Of all the idiotic, stupid, and—"

"Kelsey!" I yell. "If you don't stop talking, I swear I'm going to tell your mom about the time you borrowed her diamond earrings without asking."

Kelsey lies back in bed, grumbling. "Fine, but if you need me to beat him up with my cast, you just let me know."

"Polly, I didn't mean to spy on you," Justin says. "And I didn't tell Mr. Pritchard I met you. I just said I'd heard somewhere that Winston Academy was giving all their slots to their cheerleading squad."

"So basically you just blew our whole strategy."

"Polly, it was against the rules. It wasn't fair."

"Whatever," I say, even though I agree with him. "I've got to go. Thanks to you I have to come up with a whole new plan."

I punch the disconnect button and then collapse onto the bed next to Kelsey. The phone rings—it's Justin again—but I let it go to voice mail.

"What an idiot," Kelsey says.

"Justin's not an idiot," I say, staring at the ceiling.

"I wasn't talking about *Justin*." Kelsey nudges me, to let me know she's just kidding.

I turn and look at her. "You're not going to tell anyone about this, right? I mean, if Melinda and everyone else found out, I'd probably get banished from the Court."

"What are you talking about? You're not going to get kicked out of the Court." Kelsey looks offended. "*I'm* the one who kicks people out of the Court, and I say you're staying. Although, you do something like this again, and I might reconsider."

"Gee, thanks. Your compassion is truly amazing."

"Don't mention it." Kelsey settles back on her pillows. "How were things at the Court today?"

I shrug. "Melinda invited Jenna to eat with us."

The minute the words are out of my mouth, I regret them. Melinda has mentioned inviting Jenna to the Court several times this year, and Kelsey has always told her to forget it.

"She what?" Kelsey's voice is low. Dangerous. I figure it's a good thing for Melinda that Kelsey won't be in school tomorrow.

Kelsey grabs her cell phone from her nightstand, and soon her fingers are flying as she taps out one, two, three text messages with her good hand. I assume they're to Melinda, but I don't ask.

"Feel better?" I ask when she's finished.

"Slightly."

"You know, if you came back to school tomorrow, you could handle this in person." Kelsey seems to think this over, and I add, "Also, you could help me with try-outs tomorrow night. You could come back and be the PlanMaster."

Kelsey sighs." Polly, I told you—"

Just then Kelsey's mom enters the room carrying a tray of steaming mugs of apple cider. "Here you go, Polly." She holds out my mug and a bottle of butterscotch syrup, because she knows I like to mix some into my cider. I call it butter cider.

"You've got the weirdest eating habits," Kelsey says.

"Don't knock it till you've tried it."

After Mrs. Taylor leaves I glance at Kelsey's mug. It's a picture of a girl holding a soccer ball, and the caption reads: OUTTA MY WAY. I KICK HARD. I remember Alyssa bought it two years ago for Kelsey's birthday.

I gesture to the mug. "I didn't know you still had that."

Kelsey shrugs. "Did you think I was going to throw it away?"

"Alyssa's trying out for Groove It Up. At least, her name's on the sign-up sheet."

"Mmmmm." Kelsey makes a point of sipping her cider. Which is her way of saying she doesn't want to talk about Alyssa.

"Don't you ever miss her?"

"No." Kelsey sets her mug on her nightstand. "I never miss people who talk smack about me behind my back. And you shouldn't either."

"Come on, Kelsey. We don't know that's what she did."

"Oh yeah? Then how do you think everyone started calling you Plastic Polly?" Kelsey demands. "I'll tell you something, if Alyssa ever came near the Court, I would banish her."

I decide not to remind Kelsey that Alyssa couldn't care less about the Court. That's a big part of the reason we're not friends with her anymore. Instead, I say, "Whatever. But doesn't it ever bother you?"

"Does *what* ever bother me?"

"Having that kind of power? Don't you think it's weird that you can decide someone can or cannot eat at your table? Just because you're the most popular girl in school?"

"Weird? No. Awesome? Most definitely. And if I didn't do it, someone else would. And besides, I haven't banished anyone this year, have I? I'd say I'm the nicest popular girl Winston Academy's ever seen. Remember Brooklyn?"

Oh, boy, do I ever. After Brooklyn banished Haley, she started banishing people left and right. She reminded me of a paranoid queen who kept firing her advisers to secure her power.

When I say that to Kelsey, she says, "You see? That's

exactly the wrong thing to say. You're popular. You're not supposed to be talking about politics or any other boring things. Think clothes. Fashion. Football games. You have to be mean." Kelsey makes a funny face, but I wonder if there's a part of her that's also serious.

"I can be mean," I say, thinking about Alyssa and the choice I made last year. "I can be just as mean as you."

"Yeah, but the difference is, you're just pretending."

"And you're not?"

"No," Kelsey says matter-of-factly. "I'm training for the day when I take over the world."

Kelsey remains serious for another second before grinning. I grin back. And then we're both laughing, so hard Mrs. Taylor raps on the wall and tells us to keep it down. And I realize that even though I've sometimes wondered if I made the wrong choice, even though I haven't always liked being at the Court, I've always loved being friends with Kelsey. She may be bossy, and sometimes she says the most outrageous and crazy things, but if I had chosen differently, I would have missed her.

Just like I miss Alyssa now.

Chapter 9

✲ ✲ ✲

True Confession: I hate reality TV, but I watch it anyway, just so I know what everyone else at the Court is talking about.

On the night of Groove It Up tryouts, I'm standing outside Winston's auditorium, waiting for the delivery guy to show up with the pizzas I ordered for the planning committee.

The sky is swathed in gray and lavender, and there's a chill in the air. A strong breeze kicks up, sending fiery red leaves spinning like sparks from the maple trees. While I wait, several groups of students walk past me heading into the auditorium. A couple of boys are wearing Frankenstein masks and holding bags of candy.

Tryouts for Groove It Up are a big deal at Winston. Many students who have no intention of auditioning show up just to hang out with their friends in the auditorium. Tonight we'll go through half of the sign-up list, and then we'll finish up on Monday night.

My cell phone rings, and the name Justin Goodwin flashes on the screen. He's called three more times, apologizing profusely on my voice mail (since I refuse to answer and actually speak to him). This time I delete his message without even listening to it.

The pizza guy—a girl, actually—finally arrives with three boxes of pizza. "That's one pepperoni, one sausage, and one pesto cheese pizza," she says.

After I pay her, she hands me the boxes and says, "Are these for Groove It Up tryouts?"

I nod. "I'm the PlanMaster."

The girl gets a wistful look on her face. "I tried out for Groove It Up, back in the day. Didn't get one of the slots, though."

"I'm sorry. Thanks for the pizza." I turn away, but she stops me.

"You know what you really need to do?"

What I really need to do is get inside so we can start auditions, but instead I say, "What?"

"You should slot in someone with a great science experiment."

"Excuse me?" I say, and try not to notice that the three extra large boxes of pizza are really heavy. And *hot*.

"Yeah. I tried to tell the planning committee the year I tried out, but they didn't care. But listen, it takes talent to be a great scientist, right?"

"Well, I guess that's probably true." What is definitely true is that I'm going to drop these pizzas if I can't put them down somewhere. Where is Derek Tanner when I really need him?

"Yes, exactly! So what you need to do is find someone who likes science and give them a slot on the Talent Team. It'd be a great way to show off good science experiments."

I frown. "Isn't that what science fairs are for?"

The pizza girl's shoulders slump. "That's what the judges said the year I tried out too." She gives me a dirty look as she walks back to her car.

Inside the auditorium is a cacophony of sound. Students are sprawled in seats and chatting with their friends. One boy is testing out his tuba. The boys in the Frankenstein masks are running around throwing candy at other students.

Alyssa is huddled in the corner with a couple of girls I recognize from the choir. I pause, wondering if I should go and say something to her. Something like *Good luck* or

Break a leg. But I doubt Alyssa wants to see me, and as a judge I don't want to be accused of playing favorites.

"I'll get that," Derek says, taking the pizza boxes from me.

"Thank you." I flash him a smile that I hope tells him I'm grateful without letting him think I like him. "Can you bring those into the practice room?"

"Sure. Can I snag a slice?"

"Just one." Most students brought takeout with them to have as sort of a dinner picnic, so the auditorium smells like a combination of hamburgers, fries, and tacos.

Derek heads toward the practice room, passing Kate Newport, who approaches me. "Hey, Polly! Can I help you with anything?"

"Um . . . yeah. That would be super helpful. Let me think." This is the third time in the last twenty minutes Kate has offered to help. "Maybe you could help keep things in order out here once the judging starts." I gesture to an irritated-looking Lindsey. She's surrounded by a group of Jenna Huff's friends who are demanding access to a private practice room before their audition.

"Okay," Kate says. Before she leaves, she adds, "I saw Jenna Huff got invited to eat at the Court?" She says it like it's a question, not an observation. I'm not sure what she's asking me, so I shrug in response. Whatever Kelsey texted to Melinda last night didn't seem to work, because today Jenna sat at the Court acting like she'd belonged there all along, and that it was only because of some oversight that she hadn't been invited before. I decided not to mention it to Kelsey when we texted back and forth today. And I doubt Melinda told Kelsey she ignored her command.

I tell Kate good-bye and then tell Lindsey she can send the first act in to the judges in five minutes. Auditions are private, so they're held in a large practice room backstage. No one is allowed in except the judges, the teacher adviser, and the person or group auditioning.

Inside the practice room Melinda and Jenna are sitting at the judge's table. Melinda is now sprawled out in the middle seat, where I was sitting ten minutes ago before I went to pay for the pizza. I decide not to make a big deal about it and plunk down next to her. To the side of us Mr. Fish sits at another table, eating a slice of pepperoni pizza and flipping through a magazine.

"Pesto cheese was the only meatless option?" Melinda says, and that's when I remember she's a vegetarian. She takes a slice and shoots me an irritated look. "You couldn't have ordered something normal, like a plain cheese pizza?"

Lindsey sends the first student in—an eighth grader with flowing auburn hair who plays the violin. I wish her good luck and tell her she can start anytime. Going first is really hard. Mr. Fish told me yesterday we have ten slots available for Groove It Up—which is two more than we had last year—but still, we're not giving one away to someone who's just okay, especially not at the beginning.

But this violin player is more than just okay. She's amazing. In fact, the *Winston Times* did a story on her last month. (Once, Melinda asked me why I felt the need to read the school newspaper every week, and I said it was because I wanted to see if the gossip section mentioned me or Kelsey. That was true, but secretly I also keep track of how well the AcaSmackers are doing. At their last meet they lost to American River by two points.)

When the violin player is finished, we thank her for performing and tell her that the final Talent Team list will be posted early next week. After she leaves, I turn to Melinda and Jenna and cast my vote.

"Yes."

"No to the violin. Yes to the pesto cheese." Melinda helps herself to another slice. "It's actually one of your better ideas."

I'm surprised, but I turn to Jenna. It takes two yes votes to get a slot on the team. "What's your vote?"

"No," Jenna says.

"Really? You didn't like it?"

Jenna shrugs. "I just wasn't feeling it."

"I think we can do better," Melinda says.

Mr. Fish is staring at Melinda and Jenna with a puzzled expression on his face, like he can't figure out why they didn't vote yes. But then he shrugs to himself and goes back to his magazine.

Next up are the soccer players, who impersonate a boy band. They're calling themselves the Soccer Shakers. So they shake, and strut, and karaoke. It's funny watching them perform, but also annoying at the same time. Anyone can try out for Groove It Up, even if they're just doing it as a joke.

"Thanks, guys," I call as they leave.

I'm about to tell Lindsey to bring in the next act—I figure we don't even need to vote—when Melinda says, "I vote yes."

"Yes for me too." Jenna adds their names to the yes list.

"But they were just doing it as a joke," I say. "They weren't actually expecting to make the cut."

"I think they're funny," Jenna says.

"And cute." Melinda giggles.

"That doesn't mean they're talented," I say. "We can kiss the TV spot and the Shattered Stars concert good-bye if our team is less talented than American River's."

"Whatever," Jenna says. "The American River team always loses. Their entire school is completely talentless."

"But—"

"Polly," Melinda says in an irritated voice, "the rules say you need two yeses to make the cut. We have two yeses. Just because you're the PlanMaster doesn't mean you get to have your way all the time."

"But—" I glance over to Mr. Fish and see he's watching us closely. I say nothing and motion to Lindsey to bring in the next act, which turns out to be Kristy and the rest of the cheerleading squad. They're voted onto the Talent Team with three yeses, and they promise us they'll do a great job, even if they now only get one slot in the show.

The next three auditions are unremarkable, except for the boys in the Frankenstein masks, who offer us the rest of their candy if we'll just give them a spot on the Talent Team. Before Jenna or Melinda can say anything, I tell them thanks, but no thanks.

Then Lindsey brings in Alyssa. She's gnawing on her lip like she always does when she's nervous, and she's fidgeting with a tassel on her turquoise scarf.

"Hey, it's that ugly girl from my history class," Melinda whispers, loud enough that I'm pretty sure Alyssa hears.

"And what, exactly, is your talent?" Jenna asks, in a

voice suggesting she finds it difficult to believe Alyssa actually has one.

"I'm going to sing." Alyssa stares at Jenna and Melinda, but she won't look at me.

"Everybody cover your ears," Jenna whispers, and Melinda has to clamp a hand over her mouth to keep from laughing.

I ignore them and cross my fingers. My stomach is churning from all the pizza. For a lot of students Groove It Up is just a cool middle school event and a chance to see a Shattered Stars concert. But for students like Alyssa, I know it's so much more. It's her chance to shine in front of everyone—especially if we win and she gets to perform on *Good Morning, Maple Oaks*. I haven't heard Alyssa sing in over a year, and I wonder if she's as good as I remember. I know boys' voices change as they get older, but does that ever happen to girls?

I shouldn't have worried, though, because Alyssa is awesome. Much better than I remembered. Mr. Fish even closes his magazine so he can listen to her. My mouth is hanging open after she finishes and leaves the room.

"Yes," I croak, casting my vote. "That was amazing."

"No," Melinda and Jenna say in unison.

"No?" I turn to them. "How can you say no? Did you just hear that? It was incredible."

Jenna yawns. "I was kind of bored."

"Me too." Melinda says. "And, jeez, someone should get her a pair of tweezers for her birthday. I really wish the nobodies of this school wouldn't pester us. I don't want to be here all night."

Lindsey goes to get the next act. And I feel dread creeping through my stomach. Nobodies? Is that Melinda and Jenna's real agenda?

I slump in my seat. I can just imagine the look on Alyssa's face when she finds out she didn't make it. If she thinks I voted against her, she'll probably hate me even more than she does now.

Lindsey, looking irritated, pokes her head in. "Derek's been complaining about having to wait so long. Can I just let him in right now?"

"Sure," Jenna says. "Send him in."

We all settle back into our chairs as Lindsey leaves to find Derek. I still feel bad about Alyssa, but I'm also curious about this surprise act. Derek has been telling me for weeks how great it is, but whenever I've asked about it, he's told me I have to wait just like everyone else.

Derek saunters in carrying a carton of eggs and a tiny frying pan.

"Is he going to make us omelets, or what?" I whisper.

Melinda shushes me. "Don't be mean to your boyfriend."

"He's *not* my boyfriend."

Melinda giggles and smiles at Derek, and I wonder if she wishes Derek was *her* boyfriend.

"Those are interesting items you've got there," Mr. Fish says. "What do you plan to do with them?"

"Hey, Coach," Derek says. "I'm going to juggle them."

"Are you serious?" I say before I can stop myself, but I'm drowned out by Melinda's and Jenna's cheers.

"Go, Derek!"

Derek begins but immediately has to stop when he drops the first egg and it splats on the floor. "Sorry," he calls. "I totally had this last night."

He starts again, but it's clear that whatever skill Derek had last night has taken a vacation. He drops multiple eggs and nails himself in the face with the frying pan. I look over at Mr. Fish and see he has closed his eyes, wincing when he hears another egg drop. Finally, when the last egg splatters the floor, Derek is forced to stop, and he says, "I'm working on it, but I've almost got it. What do you think?"

"We'll let you know." Then I thank him and ask him to leave.

"Yes," Melinda says after Mr. Fish has left to find a mop.

"Yes," Jenna echoes.

"Why?" I say. "He can't juggle those eggs. He probably couldn't even make an omelet with those eggs. All he did was make a mess."

"He said he was working on it," Jenna says. "You don't have to be so mean all the time, Polly."

"Yeah," Melinda says. "Besides, he's our friend. Groove It Up won't be as much fun without him."

The dread I felt in my stomach earlier comes creeping back. Forget actual talent. It seems like Melinda and Jenna have no interest in voting for anyone unless they're part of our crowd. The popular crowd.

The rest of the night shows me I'm right. After Mr. Fish mops up the eggs, the auditions resume. As each act goes on, I can predict how Jenna and Melinda will vote based on the popularity of the students auditioning. They vote no for a small seventh grader who's actually a great break-dancer, but vote yes for the Glitter Girls—a group of Jenna's friends who perform a dance routine—even though none of them have any rhythm.

After the last act has performed, Melinda and Jenna leave. I finish off a slice of pesto cheese—Melinda's right; it's really good—and then look under greasy napkins and empty pizza boxes for the yes list. If I counted it right, Melinda and Jenna gave yes votes to five acts. That's half of the available slots.

But maybe I can change their minds, I think as I continue to hunt for the list. Maybe Monday night there will be so much talent that they'll have to take some of these acts off the list.

Lindsey enters the room, looking tired. She drops into a seat and grabs the last slice of pepperoni. "What are you looking for?"

"The yes list."

"Melinda and Jenna have it. They're posting it now."

"*Now?* But tryouts aren't done yet." I don't wait for Lindsey to answer. I dash past her, hoping to catch Melinda and Jenna, but I'm too late.

Out in the auditorium several clumps of students crowd in front of the list. Melinda and Jenna are surrounded by the cheerleaders and Glitter Girls. The Soccer Shakers look surprised, but they're cheering for Jenna and Melinda.

"Even Queen Kelsey couldn't have done a better job!" someone shouts.

"Kelsey who?" Melinda and Jenna say in unison, and everyone starts laughing.

Several other people in the auditorium aren't laughing. The violin player is wiping tears from her eyes. A girl who did a dramatic reading from Emily Dickinson is ripping the poem into shreds.

I'm searching the room, looking for Alyssa, when I hear the double doors whoosh open and see a snatch of a turquoise scarf disappear into the foyer. Quickly I cross the room, ignoring dirty looks from the kids who didn't make the Talent Team, and cheers from the kids who did.

"Alyssa, wait!" I call, but she doesn't turn around.

Outside, night has fallen. Moonlight frosts the trees, and leaves rustle in the wind. Alyssa's turquoise scarf is flapping behind her as she half-walks, half-runs toward the parking lot.

"Alyssa, please wait!"

Alyssa stops under a streetlight that glows the color of orange sherbet. She turns around. When I catch up to her, I see tiny diamond-shaped tears trickling from her eyes.

"What?" she demands. "What do you want?"

I had so much I wanted to say, but now the words seem stuck in my throat.

"I'm sorry."

"You're sorry? Yeah, right." Alyssa mimics Melinda's voice. "Oh, look. It's that ugly girl from my history class."

"I voted for you, Alyssa. I swear. But Melinda and Jenna outvoted me. That never would have happened if Kelsey were here."

"But *you're* here, Polly. And you're the PlanMaster. But

you just followed along with Melinda and Jenna, letting them rig the auditions."

"They weren't rigged," I answer automatically. Even though I agree with Alyssa, I feel the need to protect Melinda and Jenna and the whole judging process. Like Alyssa says, I'm the PlanMaster, and I'm not ready to admit that the judging committee would only vote for the popular kids. Our friends, in other words.

"They were totally rigged."

"Why?" I say, anger flaring in my chest. "Just because we didn't pick you? You don't make the cut, so now you think the whole thing is rigged?"

"I saw the list. You never should've been made the PlanMaster. You've let your new BFFs turn Groove It Up into a popularity contest."

"Melinda and Jenna are *not* my best friends."

Headlights blink in the parking lot, and I bring a hand up to shield my eyes.

"That's my dad," Alyssa says. "I have to go." Alyssa stares at me for a moment longer. "Do you really think our school can win with that list? Because if you do, you're even more deluded than I thought you were."

Chapter 10

✲ ✲ ✲

True Confession: Sometimes I wonder if my mom wishes she had a daughter who was more like her: someone determined, who always knows what she wants.

ON SATURDAY NIGHTS MOM IS IN CHARGE OF DINNER. But she hates to cook, so tonight, like most other Saturday nights, we're eating dinner at Chip's. All of the red vinyl booths are filled, and the diner smells like a combination of spicy chili, fresh-baked bread, and coffee. Outside, rain taps against the window. On the walls Chip has hung up several red-and-yellow Groove It Up banners with our school slogan: WINSTON FOR THE WIN!

Since Chip serves breakfast all day long, I always order hot chocolate and pancakes when we go out to dinner. I also order four small sides of chocolate, strawberry, butterscotch, and maple syrup. Then I dunk small pieces of pancake in one of the syrups until they're soaked through. I call it pancake fondue.

While I'm drowning a chunk of pancake in chocolate syrup, I tell Mom and Dad about the tryouts and what a disaster they were. Mom and Dad sit close together and hold hands while I talk. Dad steals bites from Mom's plate, and Mom takes small sips of Dad's coffee, because she says she only wants a little caffeine this late at night. These are the nights I like most, when neither of them are working and the three of us can just hang out.

When I've finished, Mom, who's all about the fine print, says, "Are there any guidelines stipulating who you can and who you can't vote for?"

I shake my head. "I checked *The PlanMaster's PlanMaster* this morning. It clearly states judges can vote for whoever they want. Technically we've done nothing wrong."

Which is exactly what Kelsey said when I called her this afternoon and told her what happened at tryouts. I didn't tell Kelsey about another rule I'd found, one I was pretty sure would solve my judging problem. If I had the guts to use it.

Dad snatches his coffee cup away from Mom and says, "It's wrong in spirit. It's a talent show competition, so the expectation is that the judges will vote for the most talented students."

"If that was the expectation, they should have put it in writing." Mom snatches the coffee cup back.

Mom and Dad argue for a few minutes. I doubt Mom actually thinks it's okay that Melinda and Jenna only voted for the popular kids. Mom and Dad enjoy debating each other over a million different topics, just to see who can make a better case.

Dad once told me Mom was not only the most beautiful woman he's ever met, but the smartest, too. Sometimes I wonder if I'll ever meet a boy who will say that about me, instead of having to put up with guys like Derek Tanner who think they're so cool just because they play football.

"Well then," Mom says when she and Dad have finished debating, "what are you going to do about it?"

"I don't know. Alyssa said—"

"Alyssa?" Mom interrupts. "Did she try out? She's so incredibly talented. Lynn told me Alyssa wants to study at Juilliard. I'll bet one day she'll sing on Broadway."

I grimace and sip my hot chocolate. Mom and Mrs. Grace—Lynn—are friends, and Mom doesn't understand why Kelsey and I don't hang out with Alyssa anymore. (I never told her about our fight over the Court.) And whenever her name comes up, Mom likes to talk about Alyssa's great talent. Just once I wish she'd brag about me that way. I mean, Alyssa's not even her daughter. And I am.

"Alyssa tried out," I say quickly, "and she says there's no way we can win the competition with the acts Melinda and Jenna selected. But Kelsey says—"

"'Kelsey says'?" Mom frowns. "What about what you say? You have your own voice, Polly. So far I've heard what Alyssa thinks and what Kelsey thinks. What about what *you* think?"

"I don't know what I think." I slam my hot chocolate down so hard, it sloshes over the side. "That's why I was asking for your opinion. There's nothing wrong with that."

Just like that, Mom can take a nice night out and ruin it. Just because I'm not more like her and always know exactly how I should handle things. I avoided her all day because when I woke up this morning, I saw she'd placed the application for Camp Colonial on my desk. So while she was taking a shower, I dropped the application onto her bed with a sticky note attached that said, *Tag. You're it!*

"Polly, I wasn't saying—"

Mom is interrupted by a syrupy voice calling across the diner, "Laura, Nick, I *thought* that was you!"

I turn. Mrs. Huff is standing near the cash register while Mr. Huff pays their bill.

"Oh no," Mom groans.

"I know," I say. Instantly the tension between Mom and me dissolves. In the face of the Huffs, we are united in our dislike of them.

"Girls," Dad warns, "be nice."

"*We* are always nice," Mom says.

Mr. Huff finishes paying the bill, and they start toward us. Mrs. Huff leads the way. Her chest is puffed out, her nose is tipped slightly upward, and her hands are clasped in front of her. She reminds me of a nosy chicken.

Something I've noticed about Mrs. Huff: Whenever she sees Mom, she wrinkles her nose and flutters her eyelashes as though the very sight of my mother is offensive to her.

"Laura, darling, how *are* you?"

"I'm fine, Sharon. How are you?"

"Oh, you know how it is—well, maybe you don't, actually. I know you must be so busy with work, but I'm coordinating the bake sale for Groove It Up. So much to do."

"Excuse me?" I say. "What bake sale?" I'm thinking back to our planning meetings, and I can't remember a discussion about a bake sale.

Mrs. Huff turns to look at me and blinks several times.

I get the distinct impression she wishes she could blink me out of existence. "Oh, Polly dear! I forgot, Jenna did tell me you're on Groove It Up's planning committee as well."

"Yes," Mom says before I can respond. "We're so proud that Polly is the PlanMaster. She said she's really enjoying having Jenna on her team."

Mom smiles at Mrs. Huff, and I have to bite back a laugh, because I haven't said any such thing, and never would.

"I wasn't aware there was a bake sale," I say.

"Yes, dear. Jenna told me you've needed a bit of help getting things organized. Anyway, Jenna thought it would be a good idea to sell snacks during intermission to raise more money for the school."

"Oh." I don't say anything else, because I don't want to admit that it actually sounds like a good idea.

"Where is Jenna?" Mom asks politely.

"Oh, she's with Melinda and some of the members of the Talent Team." Mrs. Huff flutters her eyelashes at me. "I'm surprised you aren't there, dear."

"Tonight is a family night," Mom says quickly.

Mrs. Huff's smile slips. "Yes. Obviously, I understand the importance of family time."

Dad, who's been following the conversation with a

wary look on his face, now says, "You know what? I think it's time for us to order our dessert. Polly, why don't you come with me and we'll refill your hot chocolate. Nice to see you, Henry," he says to Mr. Huff as we scoot out of our booth and walk past him.

"Thanks for getting me out of there," I say.

"No problem." Dad's cell rings. He checks it and says, "I've got to take this. Can you order for us?" He answers his phone and heads over to the waiting area.

Chip is brewing coffee when I plunk down at the counter. A sign by the register promises one free slice of pie to each Winston family if we win Groove It Up.

"Polly the PlanMaster," he says. "How's life treating you these days?"

"Good."

My family has been eating at Chip's every week for as long as I can remember, so when I tell him I need to order dessert, he punches in our usual fall order: two slices of pumpkin cheesecake for Mom and me, and one slice of apple pie for Dad.

I look over at Mom while Mrs. Huff talks and gestures animatedly. Mom's face is frozen in a smile that looks ready to crack at any moment. I pull my cell from my pocket and send her a text:

Want me to dream up a fake crisis to get you away from
her?

I've seen Mom pretend to receive an important text to
get out of a conversation she finds particularly tiresome.
She would never admit to it, but still, I know she does it.

"Can you hold on a sec, Sharon?" Mom says loudly.
"I need to respond to this." A second later my cell pings:

Mrs. Huff is your elder. You need to be respectful to
her. But . . . sure. Dream away. I think I'll need a fake
crisis in about ten minutes.

Chip refills my hot chocolate mug and pushes it toward
me. "You know who you should put on the Talent Team?"

"Who?"

"Some of Winston's choir kids. I heard them sing
Christmas carols last year. Man, those kids got a good set of
pipes on them, let me tell you. Especially that one girl you
used to come in here with all the time. What was her name?"

"Alyssa."

Chip nods. "Guaranteed, no one at American River
can match her voice. You should put her on the Talent
Team."

"I wish I could," I say softly, dragging my straw through a mound of whipped cream.

Mr. Huff sits down on the stool next to me. "Hello, Polly."

"Hi, Mr. Huff," I answer politely, and check my cell phone. Seven more minutes until I text Mom.

"Jenna tells me you've been struggling with Groove It Up details," Mr. Huff says. "I'm glad she's there to help you."

"Yeah, sure." I make a point of staring into my hot chocolate. Mom would kill me if she thought I was being rude, but I've had my fill of Huffs this week.

"I don't know if you know this," Mr. Huff continues, "but I'm on the fund-raising committee for Winston Academy. I don't think I need to tell you that a win at Groove It Up this year—and the exposure we'd get on *Good Morning, Maple Oaks*—would probably result in more dollars coming into the school. So as I see it, there are several things I think you can do to—"

"Henry," Dad says, coming up behind us. "How are you?"

While Dad and Mr. Huff chat, I swivel my stool away and stare out the window. The wind and the rain are beating against a Groove It Up banner Chip strung up above the door. The banner is coming undone, and looks ready to blow away unless someone sets it right.

I think about the rule I found in *The PlanMaster's Plan-Master*. The one that could solve my judging problem. I'm tired of being pushed around by everyone who thinks they know exactly what I should do as the PlanMaster. Kelsey, Alyssa, Melinda, Jenna, Mr. and Mrs. Huff, and even Chip and the pizza girl from last night all seem to have their own opinions on the subject, and none of them have any problems sharing them with me.

Pushover Polly, is that who everyone thinks I am? Have I been so great at acting like I don't have any firm opinions that everyone thinks I'll just take theirs?

For a second I remember the look on Alyssa's face after tryouts. Groove It Up is starting to feel like a giant version of the Court, with me, Melinda, and Jenna dictating who can and cannot get an invite. Is that what I really want?

But then again, why should I even care? The popular kids are my friends. This morning I received a jillion texts from people thanking me for selecting them. Shouldn't I just sit back and enjoy the ride?

But if I do, we're going to lose. Melinda and Jenna may not see that, but I do. If nothing changes, I can just imagine what tryouts on Monday night will look like:

popular kids getting put through, while the more talented but less popular kids get pushed out.

Maybe Mom wasn't being mean when she told me to find my own voice. Because when it comes down to it, as the PlanMaster *I'm* ultimately going to be held responsible for the Talent Team we select.

I lean over and tell Chip we'll be taking our order to go. Then I send Mom a text:

ATTN Mrs. Pierce: This is your daughter texting you. My fake crisis is now commencing. We must leave the diner immediately.

I gather up the bag Chip hands me and head for the door. Tonight I have a date with *The PlanMaster's PlanMaster*. Before school starts on Monday, I want to make sure my plan is perfectly within the rules.

Pushover Polly is history.

Enter Polly the PlanMaster.

Chapter 11

�   ✦   ✦

*True Confession: Sometimes I read my history textbook
even when I don't have homework.*

MONDAY MORNING I'M STANDING IN MR. FISH'S CLASS-
room holding a chilled pumpkin cheesecake.

Mr. Fish stares at me over a stack of corrected English
essays. "Isn't it a little early for pie?"

"I just thought you might like some. There's one for
now," I say, and slide another pie out of the bag. "And one
for later. I bet your daughters would *loooove* some cheesecake."

Mr. Fish leans back in his chair and crosses his arms
over his chest. "What are you up to, Miss Pierce?"

"What did you think of tryouts on Friday night?" I ask
instead.

Mr. Fish's eyes change then. They get darker. Almost like he's pulled a gate across them. "I thought they were well organized," he says slowly.

"Sure," I say, "but would you like them to be just as *well organized* tonight?"

Mr. Fish nods once, and I think he knows exactly what I'm talking about. "What exactly are you planning, Miss Pierce? And are you using these cheesecakes to buy my silence?"

I hold up a plastic fork and hand it to Mr. Fish. "Over the weekend I read *The PlanMaster's PlanMaster* cover to cover."

"And?" Mr. Fish opens up a pie and digs in with the fork.

"And the rules give the PlanMaster a lot of power over the judging and planning committee." I tell him my plan. When I'm finished, Mr. Fish is silent.

"Well?" I ask. "What do you think?"

"I think," Mr. Fish says, staring at a creamy bite of pie, "this may be the best pumpkin cheesecake I've ever had in my life."

"Does that mean you won't try to stop me?"

"Like you said, the rules state you are in charge."

"Okay, then." I turn to leave, but Mr. Fish clears his throat.

"Miss Pierce?"

I turn back. "Yeah?"

Mr. Fish almost smiles. "Good for you."

Later that afternoon I'm standing in front of the mirror that's in my locker, talking to myself. Right now I need a pep talk of epic proportions. Once I put my plan into place, there'll be no turning back. And I have to move forward. This morning when I looked at the sign-up sheet for tonight's tryouts, I noticed that everyone from the music or drama department had crossed their names off the list. It doesn't take a genius to figure out someone's telling them not to bother trying out.

"You are just as tough as Melinda and Jenna," I whisper to myself. "The way they're acting is unacceptable. You will not apologize for what you are about to do. You are doing this because you care about this school and about Groove It Up. If they get mad at you, too bad for them. Do *not* apologize. Do *not* act weak."

I practice a look in the mirror, one that I hope says *I'm tough, and don't even* think *of messing with me.*

But then I sigh and slip my cell phone from my pocket. Maybe I should call Kelsey and ask her what she thinks of my plan. I mean, I'm pretty sure she'll hate it, but maybe she'll have some ideas for what I can say to Melinda and Jenna.

But then I give myself a shake and continue with my talk:

"You do not need Kelsey's advice. You are the Plan-Master now. So go out there and—"

"Hey, Polly, what's up?"

Behind me Kate Newport is smiling and clutching a textbook to her chest. "Are you on the phone or something?" Her eyes stray to my cell.

"Uh, I was," I say quickly. "I just had to tell Kelsey something real quick."

"Cool." Kate slips a paper from her textbook and hands it to me. "I went ahead and finished all the questions for our history assignment."

"You did *all* the questions?" I look at the paper and frown. Kate and I are partners in history class. Last week we were assigned several essay questions we were supposed to divide up and answer.

"Yeah," Kate says. "I figured with Groove It Up tryouts you wouldn't have time to do it."

Why would you figure that? I want to ask, but don't. It's clear from Kate's smile she thinks she's done me a huge favor and is expecting me to thank her. Right now, though, I don't feel all that thankful.

Look, I don't love homework, but I don't exactly hate it either. History is my favorite subject, and just by glancing at the questions I can tell Kate got at least one wrong. Plus, I already did my questions last night—after I finished rereading *The PlanMaster's PlanMaster*.

But I don't tell Kate any of that. Instead I say, "Thanks. That's super helpful. You really saved me." Then I make a mental note not to let her see my homework.

"Are you heading over to the Court?" Kate asks.

"In a second, yeah."

"Cool. Well, have fun." Kate lingers for a moment, like she's waiting for me to say something.

Just then Principal Allen's voice crackles over the loudspeaker. "Attention students: I'd like to make an announcement. I've just received word from Polly Pierce, our replacement PlanMaster, that tryouts for Groove It Up this afternoon have been canceled and are rescheduled for Thursday."

Principal Allen's announcement couldn't have come at a better time. Now Melinda and Jenna will be dying to talk to me. Perfect. I quickly say good-bye to Kate and leave. I make a point of looking calm and collected as I saunter into the cafeteria. After Principal Allen's announcement everyone's going to be looking at me.

But I have to work hard to keep my smile in place when I glimpse the Court.

Because sitting at the head of the table—in Kelsey's normal spot—is Melinda. Jenna is sitting at her right, in my usual spot.

As I go through the cafeteria line, I think about what I should do. If Kelsey were here, she'd throw a fit. Because Kelsey's right. She is a lot nicer than Brooklyn was last year. But if you cross her? Watch out. So I don't know what I should do. Demand they stand up and move over?

"You're in Kelsey's seat," I say to Melinda.

Melinda puts down her soda and looks around. "Gee, I don't see Kelsey here. Jenna, do you see Kelsey anywhere?"

"I do not see her," Jenna says.

"It's still her seat, even if she isn't here."

Melinda rolls her eyes. "Jeez, Polly. Lighten up. You're acting like it's sacred space. It's just a chair in a cafeteria."

Look, a lot of people would probably think Melinda's right, that something like this is trivial. Lame middle school nonsense. They'd probably tell me to just sit down at the stupid table already and not pout because I don't get my usual seat. But those people don't know anything about life at the Court. The past couple days I've wondered if Melinda wants to stage a coup d'état—if she's trying to overthrow Kelsey as the most popular girl at Winston. And with her sitting at the head of the table, it sends a message, like Melinda's the newly crowned queen of the Court.

I stand there for another few seconds. Finally I decide I'll deal with this later, after Kelsey comes back. For now I have something more important I need to discuss with Melinda.

"What's up with that announcement?" Melinda says after I've sat down. "Why did you cancel tryouts?" Her voice sounds disapproving. "And why didn't you tell us sooner? We shouldn't have to find out along with everyone else."

I shrug. "You heard what Principal Allen said. I need more time." I give myself a final silent pep talk: *You can do this. Do NOT back down. It's now or never.*

"*We* don't need more time," Jenna says. "If *you* can't be bothered to make Groove It Up a priority, then maybe you shouldn't be the PlanMaster."

"Oh, Groove It Up is a priority, all right," I say.

Lindsey silently watches the three of us as we talk. More than anything, she's careful. She reminds me of me last year—always waiting to see who was in and who was out, before speaking. "Polly, what's going on?" she asks.

"I'll tell you what's going on." I turn to Melinda and Jenna. "What's going on is, you're fired."

"What?" Melinda says.

"Fired?" Jenna repeats. "Fired from what?"

"From the judging committee. Your services will no longer be required."

The conversations going on around the rest of the table stop. Kristy's fork is raised in midair. Derek's mouth hangs open in a surprised O.

Melinda looks confused. "Kelsey told you to fire us?"

I don't even think she said it to be mean. I think Melinda honestly can't believe I would do something like this on my own.

"So Kelsey tells you to fire us," Melinda repeats, "and the two of you get your way, just like always?"

"Kelsey has nothing to do with it. *I'm* the PlanMaster."

Next to me Jenna is pale with fury. "You can't do this," she hisses.

"Guess what, Jenna? I just did."

Jenna's eyes narrow to little slits. "You don't deserve to be the PlanMaster. You don't have a clue what you're doing. Both my sisters were the PlanMasters, and they say you—"

"I don't care what anyone in your family thinks. You're fired, and that's the way it is."

"You're kicking us off the planning committee?" Melinda looks dumbfounded.

"Nope. You're still part of the committee. You just won't be judges anymore."

"So what do you expect us to do at tryouts? Coordinate all the acts?" Jenna speaks with disdain, as though even the thought of such a thing is beneath her.

"No, I don't expect you to do that," I say. "Because Lindsey, as the Vice PlanMaster, is in charge of coordinating the acts. So she'll let you know what she needs you to do." I turn to Lindsey. "Is that okay with you?"

Lindsey looks at Melinda and Jenna and smiles. I can tell she likes it, the fact that she's been elevated, while Melinda and Jenna have been brought low.

"Works for me," Lindsey says, and goes back to her lunch.

"You can't do this," Jenna repeats.

"Of course I can," I say. "I'm the PlanMaster." My voice is so sugary, I'm probably giving myself cavities. "Unless you'd rather not be a part of the committee?"

I can see in Melinda's and Jenna's eyes that they're doing the math. Popular girls are great at doing the math. And by "math" I don't mean algebra. I mean all the little calculations we make every day to stay popular. Adding up our outfits, words, and actions and rounding them out to a social sum that will, hopefully, keep us popular.

So I bet Melinda and Jenna are probably thinking something like this: They don't like being fired. Maybe the only respectable thing to do is quit the committee. But now, thanks to their rigged judging system, a lot of the popular kids are participating in Groove It Up, and they don't want to miss out.

Melinda and Jenna glance at each other, and Jenna nods.

"We'll stay," Melinda says.

"Great. Because I have something for everyone." I dig into my backpack and pass out white envelopes to the members of the planning committee. Last night, as the second part of my plan, I came up with assignments for everyone—collecting tickets, handling the Talent Team props, set up, tear down. We're not spending any more committee meetings gossiping or fighting. It's time to get to work.

While the girls read their assignments, I feel a rush of exhilaration, like I have just accomplished a major coup. But it's short-lived when Derek turns the conversation back to the Winston Wildcats. Same old, same old. I quickly finish my salad, make up an excuse about needing to talk to Mr. Fish, and leave.

Suddenly the Court is the last place I want to be.

Chapter 12

✫　✫　✫

True Confession: I don't even like Shattered Stars'
songs, but I buy their music anyway because
everyone else likes them.

THE LAST TIME I VISITED ALYSSA'S HOUSE WAS THE DAY
before seventh grade started. Kelsey and I went over so we
could devise our middle school strategy. Kelsey said we
needed a game plan, especially since Alyssa's locker wasn't
near ours and none of us had any classes together.

Alyssa thought we were being paranoid. "We've been
going to Winston Academy since kindergarten," she said.
"This is just the middle school section. It's not a big deal."

Alyssa refused to talk about a "middle school strategy," so we ended up picking out our outfits for the
next day, singing a bunch of bad karaoke on her dad's

machine, and snacking on the back-to-school brownies Mrs. Grace had baked.

Now Mrs. Grace looks shocked to see me standing on her doorstep. "Polly!" she exclaims after she opens the front door. "It's so good to see you!" She envelops me in a hug. When she releases me, she says, "Is Alyssa expecting you?"

"No." For a second I wonder if Alyssa told her mom why we aren't friends anymore. If she had, would Mrs. Grace still look so happy to see me? "Is she home?"

"She's in her room." Mrs. Grace opens the door wide. "You know the way."

In her room Alyssa is sitting at her desk in front of her computer. "Hey, Mom, who was at the—" She stops when she turns and sees me.

"Hey." I wave slightly. "It's me."

"I can see that," Alyssa says. "What do you want?"

"Alyssa!" comes Mrs. Grace's voice. *"I have snacks for you and Polly!"*

Alyssa sighs and stands up. "I'll be right back."

My phone rings as she leaves. It's Justin with his daily apology, so I let it go to voice mail. Alyssa's room is the same as I remember. Posters of different musicals decorate her walls: *Chicago*, *The Phantom of the Opera*, *Wicked*. A tiny pair of sparkly ruby slippers still sits on her bookshelf. I was with her the day we found them at a thrift shop. There's still a glass jar of M&M's on her desk, because Alyssa always said she was incapable of doing homework without large quantities of chocolate.

I used to know every single thing about Alyssa. What boy she had a crush on. Her current favorite singer—which changed all the time, depending on her mood. What Alyssa and Mrs. Grace had fought about the day before.

But now I don't know anything about Alyssa's life. On her corkboard she has tacked up a ton of pictures. In one Alyssa is at last year's Spring Fling dance with her choir friends. In another she's rooting for the Wildcats at the homecoming game. In the background of the picture, I can see the top of the pink beanie I wore that night. Kelsey and I hadn't realized we were sitting so close to Alyssa until halftime. Then, I remember, we went out of our way to laugh longer and harder at Melinda's nasty comments, even though they weren't funny. It was like we were trying to send Alyssa a message: *We don't miss you at all.*

Also tacked on the corkboard are three tickets to a play. I don't recognize the name of the play, but I figure it must be a musical. Behind the tickets I glimpse an old picture of me and Kelsey and Alyssa. Quickly I remove the picture—

being careful not to disturb the play tickets—and sit down on Alyssa's bed.

It was taken the summer before seventh grade started. I'm standing in between Alyssa and Kelsey. I'm smiling, but Kelsey and Alyssa aren't. If I remember correctly, they'd gotten into a fight that day—over what, I can't remember anymore.

In this photo I see the me I used to be. Before I joined the Court and became popular. Before I started giving myself pep talks in front of a mirror. My hair is tied back in a ponytail and I'm wearing a T-shirt and cutoffs, something I wouldn't be caught dead in now.

The Polly I'm staring at right now—the Polly with the ponytail and the cutoffs—is she the real me?

I stand up and walk over to the mirror on Alyssa's closet door and stare at myself. The me I am today. I changed so much about myself once seventh grade started. I practiced a new voice, and a newer, more confident walk. I bought a *ton* of new clothes and jewelry. (Mom didn't seem to care, so I just went with it.) And I got a really great haircut. But does all that make me a fake? Am I really Plastic Polly? Alyssa would probably say so. Kelsey would probably say no.

I look back at the picture again. Both Alyssa and Kelsey

have always known exactly what they want and how to get it, but I'm not like that. I'm still trying to figure out what I want. Last year I decided I wanted to reinvent myself (no more bookworm with the squeaky voice) and socialize at the Court, and actually have some fun in middle school, instead of taking the Star Student test.

Because, not to brag, I'm pretty sure I would've passed it. One day in the library I pretended to be texting Kelsey while I eavesdropped on Bethany Perkins and her friend. They talked all about the test, and the questions they thought were difficult. I knew the answers to all of them.

But I don't think all that makes me a fake. I mean, I know I don't always say what I really think. But really, does *anyone* in middle school always say what they really think?

I hear Alyssa coming down the hall. I stuff the picture into my backpack so she won't see me holding it. The next time she leaves the room, I'll just pin it back up on the corkboard.

Alyssa enters carrying a tray with a plate of brownies and two glasses of milk. "We had leftovers in the fridge," she says grudgingly.

"Cool." I join Alyssa on the floor, and we eat cross-legged in silence.

"So, why are you here?" Alyssa asks again after we've finished eating.

"I moved tryouts for Groove It Up back a few days."

"I heard." Alyssa looks impatient, like she wishes I would leave.

A part of me wants to tell Alyssa that I just came to hang out, and that I want to be friends again. But I know we're past that. I know if I said sorry, Alyssa would tell me it was too little, too late.

"A lot of people crossed their names off the tryout sheet," I say instead.

Alyssa shrugs. "Of course they did. Everyone is saying the judges will only vote for the popular kids, so what's the point?"

"Then I need your help."

"*My* help?"

I nod. "I fired Melinda and Jenna as judges."

"You fired them?" Alyssa looks surprised. Then a huge smile spreads across her face. She leans forward. "How did they take it?"

"Not well. I thought Jenna was going to pass out from shock."

"I'd have paid money to see that." Alyssa starts to laugh. Then I laugh too.

Once we stop, I say, "I need judges to take their place."

"And you want me to be a judge?"

"Well, yes," I say, "but that's not all. I also need you to be my talent scout."

This is the plan: Alyssa's going to show me around the Dungeon. If the talented kids at Winston Academy won't come to me, then I'll go to them. We're going to recruit students to try out for Groove It Up. Then on Thursday we'll hold tryouts for the rest of the Talent Team. Alyssa and I will be judges. I still need a third judge, but I think I know who I can ask, so I'm not too worried about that.

It took a while to convince Alyssa to help me. I couldn't tell if it was because she didn't want anything more to do with Groove It Up or if she just didn't want to hang out with me. Finally I said, "Look, you said what Melinda and Jenna did wasn't right. Here's your chance to change things." Alyssa gave in then and said she'd help.

Early the next morning Alyssa and I meet in front of the administration building. As we walk past Principal Allen's office, Mrs. Baker, the school secretary, stops me.

"Polly? Principal Allen would like a word with you."

"Uh-oh, busted," Alyssa says.

"What do you mean, 'busted'? I haven't done anything wrong."

"Yeah, but yesterday you fired Jenna Huff. What do you want to bet that her mom has been pestering Principal Allen since the second she found out?"

I find out pretty quickly Alyssa is right, because as soon as I'm seated in front of Principal Allen, she says, "Polly, I've received some troubling phone calls. Is it true you fired a couple of the girls from the judging committee?"

"Have you been talking to Mrs. Huff?" I ask.

"Who I've been talking to isn't important. What is important is that I understand what's been going on. Did you or did you not fire them?"

"Yes. I fired them." I think about what Mom would say if she was arguing a case in front of a jury. "They were engaging in unfair judging practices."

Principal Allen looks worried. Her eyes are squinched up, and the lines on her forehead show. "If you didn't like the way Melinda and Jenna were doing things, the appropriate action would have been to discuss your feelings with them."

"Have you ever tried to discuss something with Jenna Huff—or any Huff, for that matter?"

For just a second the corners of Principal Allen's lips

tilt upward, but then she mashes them together and is all business. "Be that as it may, you can't go around firing people just because you don't like how they're doing their job."

"Actually, I can." I pull *The PlanMaster's PlanMaster* from my backpack and drop it onto her desk with a thud. Then I open it.

"It says on page eighty-three that the PlanMaster can select anyone to judge tryouts and may replace judges at any time if needed." I close the book. "I decided it was needed."

"Let me see that."

I hand Principal Allen the binder. She opens it and rifles through all the sticky notes I've attached. "You read this whole thing?"

"Twice. And I'm the one who highlighted everything."

"Impressive." She hands the binder back to me. "But I'm not sure—"

"Don't you want to win?" I interrupt, and her eyes slide over to the blank space in her trophy case.

"Yes, I do."

"Me too. And Jenna and Melinda were going to sink our chances. And according to the rules, I haven't done anything wrong. Not technically."

"Not technically," Principal Allen repeats. She doesn't look convinced. "I guess I just don't understand it. Isn't Melinda Drake one of your best friends?"

I'm quiet, because I don't know how to answer that. Melinda is the third most popular girl at Winston, right after Kelsey and me. So on the outside, I guess it does look like she's one of my best friends. But how can I explain that Melinda, someone I've hung out with every day for the past year, isn't someone I would consider a best friend? That most of the time I don't even like her?

"Well," I say slowly, "we're both popular. We both hang out at the Court." I wince, because I know I probably sound shallow.

Principal Allen surprises me by smiling, and for just a second she seems a lot younger. "I get it. Winston Academy is full of traditions. When I was your age, I used to hang out at the Court. Your mother, too."

"My mom was part of the Court?" I have a hard time picturing this. Mom always seems so serious. Even on Saturdays she usually wears her hair in a bun, just in case she has to throw on work clothes and go into the office.

Principal Allen grins. "People change a lot over the years. You'd be surprised." She seems to catch herself and stops smiling, resuming her usual firm voice. "All right,

Polly. It sounds like everything here is in order, so I won't interfere. But I would advise you to be cautious. More incidents like this, and people will begin to doubt your leadership."

After Principal Allen releases me from her office, Alyssa and I pay a visit to my locker so I can drop off my backpack. Then I start toward the staircase leading down to the Dungeon, but Alyssa stops me.

"Not yet. There's something I want to show you." Alyssa walks to the end of the hall, shoves the door open with her hip, and heads outside.

"Where are we going?" I ask when she walks around Winston's auditorium instead of stepping inside.

"You'll see."

Behind the auditorium there's nothing but a bunch of stinky Dumpsters. Standing beside them are two boys, who look like they could both use a long shower, playing hacky sack.

"Why are we back here?"

"Just watch," Alyssa whispers.

Sighing, I cross my arms and watch the hacky sackers. Ten minutes before the bell rings and I'm stuck in a smelly no-man's-land with two grungy boys who have nothing better to do with their lives than haphazardly kick a small ball with their feet.

Except as I watch them, I realize there's nothing haphazard about it at all. The two boys are bouncing and bopping their hacky sack back and forth in a routine. After a few minutes they add in another ball. In perfect unison the two of them are kicking, jumping, spinning—keeping the hacky sacks from touching the ground with choreography so clean I think even Kristy Palmer would be impressed.

"Wow."

Alyssa nods. "I know."

"How did you know they'd be back here?"

"Most people know they're back here. You need to get out around campus more."

I start to protest but stop. The truth is, I spend most of my time, when I'm not in class, at the Court, or hanging out in the English hall by my locker. I rarely have to leave my locker to go find someone. People come to me. That probably sounds like I'm bragging, but I'm really not. That's just how it is.

I clear my throat, and one of the boys turns around. Then he nudges the other boy, who also turns around.

"Oh, dude!" the second boy says. "It's Plastic— I mean, shoot, it's Polly Pierce!" He turns red. "Sorry."

"No problem," I say. "What's your name?"

"Kai, and this is Aidan."

"Nice to meet you guys. Do you know I'm the Plan-Master for Groove It Up this year?"

Kai and Aidan look at me strangely. "Everyone knows that," Aidan says.

"Then you also probably know that tryouts are in a few days."

Kai shrugs. "Yeah, so?"

"So, I want you two to try out. I think you're really talented."

Kai and Aidan stare at each other like they're not sure they should believe me.

"I mean it. Tryouts are on Thursday, and I'd really like it if you could come." In my head I imagine myself whipping out a business card that reads POLLY PIERCE, PROFESSIONAL PLANMASTER, and saying, "Call me anytime, dahling!"

"I heard tryouts this year were a sham," Kai says, "that unless you were in with the Court, not to bother."

"Well, it's not like that," I say. "At least, not anymore."

"So you're saying there's, like, a new sheriff in town?" Kai grins at me.

"Yeah." I grin back. "I guess there is."

✩ ✩ ✩

True confession: I've never hung out in the Dungeon. I've never had any reason to. I'm not involved with the choir or drama club, and I'm not friends with anyone who is—so I feel a little nervous at lunch when Alyssa and I meet at the top of the staircase leading into the Dungeon.

"One thing before we go," Alyssa says.

"Shoot."

Alyssa looks uncomfortable. "I know that the Court and you and Kelsey and all your friends are a big deal and everything, but people in the Dungeon don't really care. It's different down there."

We walk down the stairs, and I'm struck by how different it really is. I'm not sure what I expected—a sad, cold, and gray place? But instead, the air is warm and musty. The walls are painted a cheery yellow, and clumps of students are relaxing in the hallway, eating lunch and laughing with their friends. I can even hear a few students singing in one of the practice rooms.

"Do people practice at lunchtime?" I ask.

Alyssa nods. "Any time they can. A lot of times I join them."

As we walk down the hall past several more practice

rooms, I notice a classroom where orange twinkle lights hang from the ceiling. In the corner a stuffed scarecrow sits on a bale of hay next to a pile of pumpkins.

"That's Mrs. Marsden's room," Alyssa says, following my gaze. "She always decorates according to the season. You should see it in December." Alyssa glances at me and quickly stops talking. Is she wondering—like I am—if we'll still be speaking after Groove It Up is over? Or will we go back to pretending like the other one doesn't exist?

We continue down the hall, and several students say hi to Alyssa. Their eyes flick over to me, and then they give Alyssa a questioning look as if to say, *What are you doing with her?* Which is funny, because upstairs it was the exact opposite. As we walked the halls, people looked at me like they couldn't figure out why I was bothering to talk to Alyssa.

We stop, and Alyssa knocks on the door of a practice room. "Hold on a minute," comes a voice from inside.

While we wait, a girl walks up to us. "Hey, Alyssa, can you tell me again about that warm-up technique your new voice coach taught you?" She stops when she finally notices me. "Oh, hey. I didn't realize you were friends with Polly."

Alyssa and I both glance at each other. I don't think either of us knows how to answer that. Winston has a huge middle school section, so there are a lot of kids here who probably don't realize Alyssa and I were ever friends. For some reason this makes me sad.

Alyssa promises the girl that she'll talk to her later, and after she's gone, I ask, "You have a new voice coach?"

"Yeah. I got tired of Lady Onion Breath."

We laugh. Then my cell phone pings with a text message from Kelsey:

You fired Melinda and Jenna? Are you out of your mind?

I'm surprised it took Kelsey this long to text me. I figured Melinda would tattle text on me the minute I left the Court yesterday.

I text back:

Possibly. I'll call you after school.

"Who was that?" Alyssa asks after I stick my phone into my pocket.

"Kelsey."

"How's she doing?" She looks genuinely concerned.

"Good. She's home from the hospital. I'm going over there after school today. Want to—" I stop. For one second I had forgotten that Kelsey and I aren't friends with Alyssa anymore. I was going to invite Alyssa to come along.

Alyssa stops smiling. I know from her perspective it probably feels like I chose Kelsey over her, but that wasn't it. That day, I was choosing the Court, and popularity, and everything I wanted.

Or at least, everything I thought I wanted.

The door opens, and a boy walks out. "Go on in," he tells Alyssa. "They're almost finished."

Inside the practice room two twin girls with long black dreadlocked hair are standing on a small stage, singing. But they're not singing in the diva-like way that Alyssa sings. They're rapping. I keep trying to catch the words, because they sound familiar.

"Wait . . . is that—are they rapping to *Hamlet*?"

Alyssa nods. "That's Tasha and Dominique. They call themselves the Shakespeare Twins. Brilliant, right?"

"Totally brilliant." I stare at the girls. Tasha and Dominique. I'm pretty sure their names were originally on the sign-up list and were crossed off yesterday.

"Hey, Alyssa," calls one of the girls. "No outsiders allowed." Her gaze flicks over to me, then back to Alyssa like I'm not even there. Or like I'm someone she can't stand, even though I'm pretty sure we've never met.

"I know, Tasha," Alyssa says, "but I wanted Polly to see

you guys. We'd like you to come try out for Groove It Up."

Tasha crosses her arms in front of her chest. "I heard no one from drama had a chance of making it into Groove It Up this year."

"Things are different now," I say, stepping closer to the stage, "and I'd really like you to try out."

Tasha looks at me and seems to consider this. "Is it true you fired Melinda Drake and Jenna Huff as judges?"

I feel something in my stomach tighten. "You heard about that?"

"Oh yeah. The whole school is talking about it. Man, there are a lot of people not happy with you right now."

"Great," I say. Then I add, "Yeah, it's true. I fired them."

Tasha turns to Dominique, and a silent look passes between them. "Then we'll definitely be there," Dominique finally answers.

Alyssa and I leave—she says there's a gymnast named Betsy she wants me to meet. We get sidetracked, though, because people keep stopping to talk to Alyssa. One girl wants to know how Alyssa did on her math test. A boy hanging out in Mrs. Marsden's room wants Alyssa to give a message to someone named Angelica. A couple girls sitting in the hallway ask if Alyssa has plans for Halloween next week.

I stand silently next to her as she answers each question, and I feel strange. All this time I guess I imagined Alyssa down here in the Dungeon by herself, a loner starved for friendship. I think back to all those photos Alyssa has tacked to her corkboard. I'm ashamed to admit this, but I guess a part of me assumed Alyssa hasn't been happy this past year, not without me and Kelsey. But as I watch her talk and laugh with everyone down here, I can see that's not the case.

Don't get me wrong, I'm glad Alyssa is happy. But if she's had such a great year, I can't help but wonder, has she missed me at all?

Chapter 13

✡ ✡ ✡

True Confession: Every day I stand in front of my closet door and ask myself, "What would a popular girl wear today?"

EVERY MIDDLE SCHOOL HAS A DRESS CODE. SURE, SOME schools have official dress codes and make you wear gross uniforms, but that's not what I'm talking about. I mean, there can be several different unofficial dress codes at one school.

Like at Winston Academy if you're a Court girl, you probably wear strappy sandals and flippy skirts. Down in the Dungeon, I've noticed the girls have a dress code of their own: long, flowing skirts, peasant blouses, and brightly colored scarfs.

I think about this as I stand in front of my closet one

morning, trying to decide what to wear. For the past few days—ever since tryouts for Groove It Up finished—I've been avoiding the Court and eating lunch with Alyssa in the Dungeon.

Kate Newport served as the third judge—you should've seen the look on her face when I asked her—and overall, tryouts went really well. Kai and Aidan, the Shakespeare Twins, and Betsy the gymnast all showed up and were voted onto the Talent Team. Alyssa and I mostly voted the same way. Kate usually waited to cast her vote until after Alyssa and I voted. She didn't seem to care all that much who made the cut. She just seemed happy to be included.

The only people not happy with the tryouts were Melinda and Jenna, and they started giving me the silent treatment at the Court. Since listening to Melinda and Jenna ignore me gets annoying (and Lindsey seems nervous every time she talks to me), I've started eating lunch with Alyssa in the Dungeon.

I pull a blue skirt from my closet. I feel out of place wearing my clothes in the Dungeon. No one else down there dresses like me. Plus, it's hard sitting on the floor of Mrs. Marsden's classroom in a shorter skirt. I decide against the skirt and put it back in my closet.

The first day that Alyssa and I ate lunch together, we

mostly talked about Groove It Up (and we ignored the weird looks from everyone else in Mrs. Marsden's room). But slowly we've started talking about other stuff too. We discuss the novels we're reading—something I can't talk to Kelsey about, since she thinks reading is a waste of her time. (Right now I'm reading *Little Women* for the book report in Mr. Fish's class.) Alyssa also told me she's trying out for the lead in the school play this spring, and that last year she had a huge crush on Derek Tanner, but he never noticed her, even though she sat next to him in three classes.

I didn't have the heart to tell her that Derek—who barely speaks to me now that he's made it onto the Talent Team—isn't all that interesting, so instead I said, "Are you serious? You should have told me. I could have introduced you."

Alyssa fell silent, suddenly seeming absorbed in her peanut butter and banana sandwich, and I realized how rude I probably sounded. Because for one thing, last year Alyssa and I weren't even speaking to each other. And second, things that seem normal to me, like hanging out with the cheerleaders and the football players, are out of reach for Alyssa.

Sometimes it feels like Winston Academy is made up of several small countries (the Court, the Dungeon, and many other cliques) with strict rules in place to keep outsiders from breaching the boundaries. I wonder if it's like that at other middle schools.

While I'm hunting through my closet, my fingers brush against a white flowing blouse I forgot I had. I pull it out and find the long skirt Mom made me buy last month for Grandma Pierce's birthday party. After I put them on, I rustle through my dresser for the one scarf I own—a sparkly light green one Alyssa and I found at a thrift shop two years ago.

I dig through my jewelry box and put on the dangly silver earrings that Kate insisted I borrow last week after I told her I thought they were cute. Then I stare at myself again in the mirror. I look almost exactly like some of Alyssa's friends.

It occurs to me that if I really want to be like the girls in the Dungeon, I could ask Mom to take me to see a few musicals. I think I could also—

My eyes fall on the picture of me, Alyssa, and Kelsey. The one from Alyssa's room I forgot to stick back on her corkboard. It's been sitting on my dresser ever since. I'm still standing in between Alyssa and Kelsey, with my ponytail and my T-shirt and cutoffs. Then I flick my eyes back to the mirror.

Who am I kidding? I hate musicals. And the flowing

blouses and skirts may look cute on the girls in the Dungeon, but right now I personally feel like I'm wearing bed sheets. If I wear this outfit today, I'll be itching and sweating before the first bell rings.

But if I wanted to, I could do it. I could turn myself into a clone of the Dungeon girls. I'm great at making myself over. I look back at the picture. I've done it once already, haven't I? And if I did it again, what would people call me then? Broadway Polly? It doesn't have quite the same ring as Plastic Polly.

I stare at the picture a while longer, then decide to change into something that's more "me." Whatever that is.

Actually, Plastic Polly is the perfect nickname, I think as I unwind the scarf from around my neck.

Because I *am* fake.

When I get to school, the hallways are festive. Tonight is Halloween, and a few students are wearing their costumes, even though it's against the rules. A group of boys are wearing silver tuxedos—Shattered Stars' trademark look— and singing. A boy dressed as Dracula comes screaming down the hall, scaring a girl so badly *she* screams and drops her textbooks. Another girl is passing out candy to anyone who stops by her locker.

I'm spinning my combination lock when I hear Alyssa come up behind me and say hi. When I turn around, I see she looks a little nervous. "Tasha, Dominique, and I are going to a harvest festival at the community center tonight. Want to join us?"

Alyssa smiles shyly, and I know she's offering me something. A friendship outside of Groove It Up and a few lunches in the Dungeon. A chance to start over.

"I'd really like to, but I can't," I tell Alyssa truthfully. "But could you come with me somewhere? Kelsey and I were supposed to go to Kristy Palmer's Halloween party—"

"I am *not* hanging out with a bunch of cheerleaders."

"You didn't let me finish," I say.

Kelsey and I *were* supposed to go to Kristy's Halloween party, but Mrs. Taylor said Kelsey can't go because of her injuries. Kelsey sent me a ton of livid texts last night, so I texted her back that I'd skip the party and hang out with her at her house and pass out candy. I'm bummed, because I worked really hard on my costume, but I'd rather be with Kelsey.

After I tell Alyssa all that, I add, "And Kristy isn't that bad." Because she's really not. She doesn't join in with Melinda and Jenna when they ignore me. And yesterday in history class she leaned over and said she was glad I'd fired Melinda and Jenna. "I want to win," she whispered fiercely. "American River can suck my snobby private school toenails."

"Yeah, right," Alyssa says now. "I'm sure Kristy and all your stuck-up Court friends are just a bundle of fun."

I ignore that and say, "You could come with me to Kelsey's house." I don't actually know if that's true or not. I don't know how Kelsey would react to seeing Alyssa. Not well, I guess. I deliberately haven't mentioned that I've been hanging out with Alyssa whenever Kelsey and I have talked or texted this week. But I want Alyssa to know her invitation means something to me.

"I don't think so." Alyssa turns like she's going to walk away.

"Okay," I say quickly, "but maybe we could hang out tomorrow after school?"

"Um, I can't," Alyssa says. "I have a history test I have to study for."

"Okay." I decide not to remind Alyssa that we have the same history teacher, just during different periods, so I know that test isn't until next week. "Maybe another time?"

"Sure, yeah," Alyssa says, and walks away.

I turn and angrily stuff my backpack into my locker, ignoring Kate Newport when she approaches and offers me a handful of candy corn. Same old Alyssa. She expects me to drop everything for her, but she won't change her plans for me, probably because she thinks her friends are better—and less shallow—than mine.

And she thinks *I'm* the stuck-up one?

Halloween is my favorite holiday. Not because of the candy, or because I like spiders and blood and guts and stuff. (Gross!) Nope, I like Halloween because it's the one night in the year when I can pretend to be anyone I want and no one can call me fake.

Last year I dressed up as a butterfly. I had shiny, sparkly wings and a glittery face mask. Everyone liked my costume, except for Brooklyn Jones, who said it was "pretty but kind of immature." So this year I wanted to pick out a costume that said, *Now here's a girl who's mature and sophisticated. Here's a girl who's in control and worth talking to.* So I decided to be Cleopatra. Besides my costume, which came with a really cool black wig, Mom let me buy chunky gold jewelry and gold strappy sandals.

When Mom and I pull up at Kelsey's house, I see candle-lit pumpkins lining the walkway, and spiderwebs hanging from the roof. I tell Mom I'll see her in a few hours, straighten my wig, and hop out of the car. A couple of boys dressed as Jedi Knights from *Star Wars* stand outside the front door while Kelsey and her little sister, Molly, drop candy into their outstretched pillowcases.

After they've left and I'm inside, Kelsey slams the door. She's got a murderous look in her eyes, and she's holding up her hot-pink cast like she'd like to smack someone with it. "Why did you bother dressing up?" Kelsey raises her voice and calls out, "It's not like we get to *go* anywhere."

"I heard that," comes Mrs. Taylor's voice from upstairs. "And I'm not discussing it any further. You're not leaving this house until you're well enough to go back to school."

Kelsey rolls her eyes and leads me and Molly into the kitchen. "Want some pizza?"

"Do you have pepperoni?"

"No, and what do you care?" Kelsey hands me a slice of plain cheese. "You'd just pick them off anyway." She slams the pizza box shut and checks her cell phone. While I silently watch, she sends off a couple of texts and mutters to herself.

"Text me back," she commands her phone.

We stare at her cell. Nothing happens.

"Who's supposed to text you back?" I ask.

"Melinda. Kristy. Lindsey. Kate Newport. Someone, anyone." Kelsey plunks down in front of the breakfast bar. "It's the most important party of the fall, and I want to know what's going on." She frowns at her phone. "I can't *believe* no one's texting me back."

"Maybe they can't hear you over the music," I say, and Kelsey scowls in response.

The doorbell rings, and I offer to get it since Kelsey's in such a rotten mood. When I open the door, I'm greeted by a little girl dressed as a ladybug. Her mom stands behind her.

"Trick or treat!"

"Happy Halloween!" I hand her a couple pieces of candy. After that several other groups of trick-or-treaters arrive and I'm busy passing out candy. Once the coast is clear, I head back inside and find Kelsey and Molly in the kitchen. Molly's standing still while Kelsey is attempting to zip up Molly's pirate princess costume with one hand.

"Need help?" I ask.

"Yeah."

Once I've zipped up the costume, Kelsey says, "Molly's telling me about a boy in her class." She turns back to her sister. "Okay, go on."

"And then he called me a poopy head," Molly says in a teary voice. "And then he pushed me down into a puddle."

"Did you tell the teacher?"

Molly nodded. "But she said she didn't see it, and that he was probably just teasing me because he likes me."

"That is unacceptable," Kelsey says. "The next time he pushes you, I want you to hit him back."

I glance toward the staircase, wondering if Mrs. Taylor can hear us. I always wanted a sister—I would've even baby-sat for her, no matter how annoying she was. And I'm pretty sure you're not supposed to tell one little kid to hit another little kid.

But when I say that to Kelsey, she says, "Why not? Molly told a teacher, and the teacher won't do anything about it." Kelsey holds up her good hand. "Okay, Molly, I want you to make a fist. . . . No, not like that. Don't tuck your thumb under your fingers. Look at how I'm doing it. . . . Good. Okay, next time he does anything, I want you to haul off and punch him as hard as you can. Right in the face."

"Molly!" comes Mrs. Taylor's voice. "Are you ready to go trick-or-treating?"

Molly grabs her candy holder—an orange plastic pumpkin—and tells us good-bye. I walk her to the front door. "Maybe next time instead of punching him, you could tell a different teacher," I whisper to her while Mrs. Taylor hunts for her jacket.

After they leave, I walk back into the kitchen. "Don't you think you're being a little harsh, telling her to hit another kid?"

"No, I don't. She has a right to defend herself. If someone gives you grief, you give it right back to them. And speaking of which"—Kelsey crosses her arms—"what's this I hear about you hanging out in the Dungeon?"

The doorbell rings then, and I hurry to get it, mostly so I don't have to answer Kelsey right away. After I pass out candy to a couple boys dressed as Spider-Man and Superman, I go back into the kitchen. "How do you know I've been hanging out in the Dungeon?" I ask, although I'm pretty sure I know the answer.

Kelsey shrugs. "Melinda texted me."

"Melinda texted you. Awesome. How many times a day does Melinda text you to tattle on me? And I'm surprised she cares. She's barely speaking to me at the Court."

"So your answer is to just run away and hide out with the dorks in the Dungeon?"

"The people in the Dungeon aren't dorks. Alyssa hangs out there."

Kelsey raises her hand to shush me. "Don't go there, Polly."

"Why not? She used to be our best friend."

"Yeah, *used to be*. Then she turned into a backstabbing gossiper. Has she apologized? I'll bet she hasn't, has she?"

"Kelsey, come on. We haven't apologized either."

"Us, apologize? For what? She's the one who went around calling you Plastic Polly behind your back."

Kelsey has always said it's Alyssa's fault, for not returning my phone calls and for calling us names behind our backs. But after the first week of seventh grade, almost every middle schooler at Winston knew my name. I wonder now how intimidating that might have felt to Alyssa.

Sometimes I wonder if I should just apologize. For choosing the Court over Alyssa (even though *not* choosing the Court would have meant not choosing Kelsey). For not agreeing to eat lunch with Alyssa every now and then. For letting our friendship just slip away and never doing anything about it.

The doorbell rings again. Kelsey tells me to go ahead and answer it, and I know the conversation is over. I pass out candy to two boys who inform me they're dressed as Dr. Jekyll and Mr. Hyde.

Sometimes this past week I've felt like I've been one version of myself with Alyssa and another version of myself with Kelsey. Like I have two separate Polly costumes. With Kelsey I talk about the boys I like and we have late-night text-a-thons when we can't sleep, and she always makes me laugh with all the crazy things she says. With Alyssa we talk about books and our love of thrift shops (I still go to them;

I just never tell anyone at the Court), and I love to hear Alyssa sing or talk about how one day she wants to be in a musical in New York.

Kelsey and Alyssa are two of the most different people I know, but they have one thing in common: They're both incredibly stubborn. Neither of them knows the first thing about apologizing.

Kelsey will be back at school next week, after Groove It Up is over. What am I supposed to do then? Go back to pretending like Alyssa doesn't exist? I don't want to do that, but since Kelsey and Alyssa can be enormous grudge holders, I'm not sure how I can be friends with both of them at the same time.

Back in the kitchen Kelsey's still grumbling about Melinda not texting her back with updates, and a thought occurs to me.

"Do you text Melinda a lot for updates?"

"If she doesn't text me first." Kelsey gives me an accusatory stare. "I need *someone* to keep me informed. You're supposed to be my eyes and ears while I'm gone, Polly, but every time I ask you what's going on at the Court, you change the subject."

I don't know why I haven't told Kelsey that I think Melinda is scheming to overthrow her, or that Jenna is still eating at the Court. Maybe because Kelsey would say that, as her second in command, it's up to *me* to hold the line while she's gone.

For a minute I consider telling Kelsey I don't want to be a part of the Court anymore, that I've had it. That she can take her popularity—my popularity—and shove it. That I'm going to spend the rest of eighth grade hunkered down with Alyssa in the Dungeon.

But that's not what I really want. I don't want to choose Alyssa over Kelsey. I don't want to have to choose at all. I want to be friends with both of them.

Why is that so much to ask?

Chapter 14

✼ ✼ ✼

True Confession: Last month for my mom's birthday I baked her a cake. But when she called to tell me she'd be working late, I pretended like I'd forgotten about her birthday. Then I tossed the cake into the trash.

AFTER I RETURN HOME FROM SCHOOL THE NEXT DAY, Mom texts me saying she won't be home until later. Then Dad texts me, saying he has a meeting and not to wait up for him. I flip on an episode of *Chef Sherry* and start zoning out while she demonstrates how to make cupcakes from leftover Halloween candy.

Today Alyssa said she couldn't eat lunch with me because she was practicing a song with some of her choir friends. I told her it was fine and that I'd just eat at the Court, but I wondered if she'd still have been busy if I'd gone to the harvest festival with her last night.

My phone rings. It's Justin again. I think this is the tenth time he's called. As the phone continues to ring, I look around at the empty living room. I could spend the afternoon watching more episodes of *Chef Sherry*. Or I could actually talk to someone.

"Hey."

"Oh, Polly, hi." Justin sounds caught off guard. "I didn't think you—I mean, I was just going to leave a message."

"So in other words you called me but you weren't actually planning on talking to me?" I settle back into the couch.

"Yes," Justin says. "I had absolutely no interest in talking to you whatsoever."

I can't help it. I laugh. And then Justin laughs too.

"But really, I am sorry," Justin continues. "So sorry. I really did try to tell you."

"Yeah, great job with that," I say, and I can't keep the smile out of my voice. "You're a master communicator."

"You wouldn't let me get a word in. It's not my fault you had a large case of logorrhea."

"Logor-*what*? What does that mean?"

"It means you wouldn't stop talking. You got a case of verbal diarrhea."

"Verbal diarrhea? Wow, you really know how to apologize to a girl, don't you?" Why is it with boys, no matter how smart they are, that the conversation often turns to bodily functions?

"Polly, can you hold on for a second?" I hear Justin speak, but it's muffled, like he put his hand over the phone. Then I hear him say, "Thanks, Mr. Fish."

"Are you at Winston?"

"Yeah. I had to drop a couple things off before our dress rehearsal tonight. Mr. Fish wants a list with the final order of our acts."

"Oh, shoot." I sit up. Tonight is the dress rehearsal for American River's Talent Team. Winston's is tomorrow afternoon, and Mr. Fish wanted a list of the order of our acts so he could put it in the Groove It Up program. I told him he'd have ours before I left for the day. Lindsey gave me the list during lunch, and I tucked it into my math textbook, which is currently sitting in my locker.

I grab my backpack and head for the door. "Will he be there for a few minutes? I need to give him our list too."

"Are you at Winston?"

"No, but I only live a few minutes away. I have to go." I punch the disconnect button and zip out the door.

Outside I notice several neighbors have stuck lawn signs supporting Winston's Talent Team in their front yards. The sky is overcast, and I shiver, wishing I'd thought to bring my jacket. The barren branches of the maple trees stretch to the sky like skeleton hands. As I squelch through mud and fallen leaves, I'm thankful I finally traded in my flippy skirt and sandals for jeans and boots.

After a quick trip to my locker, I head to Mr. Fish's classroom with the list. Justin is standing outside the door.

"I just wanted to apologize one more time."

"Okay," I say. "Apology accepted."

After I hand the list to Mr. Fish, he wants to go over several last-minute details. So I open my backpack and pull out the clipboard I borrowed from Mom. With Groove It Up only two days away, there have been so many details to remember that I finally made a to-do list, which is now three pages long.

"You reserved practice rooms?" Mr. Fish asks.

I check my list. "Yes, and I made sure each member of the Talent Team has a pass for their afternoon classes tomorrow so they can practice before the dress rehearsal."

"Good." Mr. Fish nods. "What about the bake sale?"

"Jenna Huff and her mom are taking care of that. They'll deliver the snacks to the auditorium Saturday morning. Also . . ." I pause and check my list. "I sent out e-mails to everyone on the planning committee with last-minute instructions. And I sent a school-wide e-mail requesting that everyone wear Winston's school colors to Groove It Up."

"Great idea." Mr. Fish checks his own to-do list. "I also need to call Zack Wilson, the emcee. He left me a voice mail a couple days ago asking what time to show up on Saturday, and I forgot to call him back."

"Don't worry about it. We e-mailed back and forth last night, and he's good to go."

We go over several more details until Mr. Fish is satisfied that everything is in order. "You have a real talent for event coordination," he says as I leave.

Outside in the hallway Justin is studying a note card.

"You sure seem to like those things," I say, tapping the card.

Justin shrugs. "I have an Academic Smackdown meet coming up."

"You're an AcaSmacker?"

"Is that what you guys call it? At my school we call ourselves the Eggheads." Justin stuffs the note card into his pocket. "I have a couple hours to kill before our dress rehearsal starts. Want to grab something to eat at that diner across the street?"

"You mean Chip's?" I think about my empty house and figure, why not? It's not like I have any reason to be home.

At Chip's we have to wait to be seated. Justin looks at the posters rooting for a Winston Academy win at Groove It Up. "Wow." He whistles. "I probably shouldn't mention I'm the PlanMaster for American River, should I?"

"No," I whisper back. "That would probably be a bad idea. Chip might charge you double."

Chip leads us to a table next to the door, so every time someone walks in, we get a blast of chilly air. We both order slices of pumpkin cheesecake and hot chocolates. Justin also orders slices of a lemon tart and chocolate cake. When our orders arrive, he practically inhales the lemon tart before I've even picked up my fork.

"Hungry much?" I say.

Justin shrugs. "So how are things going, being the PlanMaster?"

My cell pings once, then twice, and I reach into my pocket. But then I figure it's Kelsey. I don't feel like reading more texts about how I'm messing up, so I decide not to check it.

"Well," I say, "that's classified. I could tell you, but then I'd have to kill you. You are the enemy, after all."

"Yes, I am the enemy," Justin says matter-of-factly, glancing again at the pro-Winston banners. "Maybe that should have been my slogan for the PlanMaster election."

He finishes off his pumpkin cheesecake in three bites and then spreads his hands wide. "Justin Goodwin: Number one enemy of Winston Academy."

I lean forward, ignoring another ping from my cell. "Are you saying you have to get elected to be the PlanMaster at your school?"

"Yeah." Justin nods. "For the whole planning committee, actually. The elections are held the first week of school, along with the elections for student council. It's a really big deal."

"Oh." Suddenly it seems like such a stupid tradition, the fact that the members of the Court automatically get to plan Groove It Up. But when you're popular, sometimes it feels like things get handed to you on a silver platter. Whether or not you deserve them.

"How have things been going for you?" I ask Justin.

"Honestly?" Justin's green eyes seem tired behind his glasses. "I'll be kind of glad when it's over. It's been fun but kind of stressful."

"I don't know *what* you're talking about," I say, rolling my eyes at him. "What could *possibly* be stressful about planning Groove It Up?"

Justin polishes off the last of his chocolate cake and leans back in the booth. "Well, I could tell you, but it's classified, so I'd have to kill you. You *are* the enemy."

We laugh, and Justin holds out his hand. "May the best man win?"

"May the best school win," I say.

We're shaking hands when I feel a chilly blast of air from behind. Then I hear Melinda's cold voice. "Why are you hanging out with American River's PlanMaster?"

I turn. Melinda and Jenna are standing behind me. Today Melinda is wearing a drab orange-and-green shirt. She sort of resembles a moldy pumpkin.

And both Melinda and Jenna are staring at me like they've just smelled a rat.

Justin looks from me to Melinda and Jenna. "Um, it's classified?" He makes a small attempt at a laugh, but no one joins him.

"We were just going over last-minute details." My voice is squeaky. And defensive, even though I know Justin and I haven't done anything wrong.

"Oh, really." Melinda smiles at me. A smile that reminds me of the way a snake looks at a rabbit.

Right before she eats it.

Melinda and Jenna get seated in the booth behind Justin, making it difficult for us to talk. Melinda texts away on her phone. Jenna loudly complains about the service and sends her slice of apple pie back to the kitchen two times—first because it's too cold, then because it's too hot.

I don't have to wonder who Melinda texted, because pretty soon my cell starts pinging every two seconds, and I figure she's been tattle texting on me to Kelsey. Finally I tell Justin I have to leave.

"I have to do damage control," I whisper, glancing at Melinda and Jenna.

"Okay," Justin says. "See you at Groove It Up?"

"Deal. I'll be the one holding the trophy over my head," I say as I slide out of the booth.

"No, you won't," Justin calls as I walk out the door.

Outside, pink clouds dot a gray sky, and my breath puffs out in frosty Os. I shiver and pull my cell phone from my pocket, intending to call Kelsey back and tell her that I swear—this time—I didn't spill any secrets about Groove It Up to Justin. Except the texts weren't from Kelsey. They were from Mom, which go from anger that I'm not home to flat-out panic that I'm not texting or calling her back. The last one reads:

Just got a call from Mrs. Huff. Leave the diner immediately. You are in BIG trouble.

I text back:

On my way.

I slip my cell back into my pocket. Great. Instead of tattle texting to Kelsey, Melinda and Jenna texted Mrs. Huff, the biggest gossip in Maple Oaks. I practically run home, hoping Mrs. Huff didn't completely ruin my night.

But I'm too late. At home Mom, who decided to leave work after all and surprise me with a gift card to a fancy restaurant one of her clients gave her, is livid. We're standing in the kitchen. The application for Camp Colonial sits on the breakfast bar, right next to the phone book. Apparently she was about to start calling hospitals when I finally texted her back.

"Okay, I'm sorry," I say for about the twentieth time. "And why are you using the phone book, anyway? You could've just looked up the number online."

I guess that was probably not the right thing to say, because Mom's face turns slightly purple, and a few hairs spring loose from her bun. "Do you think this is *funny*, young lady? Because I think you get a lot of privileges around here." Mom starts ticking things off on her fingers. "You get a cell phone. A very expensive one, I might add. You get a credit card in case you need it. We don't give you a lot of grief over chores. I'd say we're pretty lenient. And *this* is how you repay us?"

I stare sullenly back at her. I want to tell her I wouldn't need the phone, or the credit card, if she was around more often. Or that she doesn't have to get on me about chores, since I keep things neat anyway.

"You know the rules, Polly. After school you come straight home. Otherwise you call me and *ask* for permission to go out."

"I'm sorry. I totally forgot. I had to—"

"I had no idea where you were. Then I have to get a phone call—from Sharon Huff, of all people—telling me that my daughter is at a diner, with a boy. Do you know how that felt, listening to that woman insinuate that I don't know how to take care of my own daughter?"

"Who cares what Mrs. Huff says? Aren't you the one who's always telling me I shouldn't care so much about what other people think?"

"Do you do this often?" Mom demands. "You're not allowed to date, and you know that—"

"It was *not* a date. Justin is—"

"—so for you to sneak out behind my back and—"

"Sneak out?" I interrupt. "Are you kidding? You'd

have to actually be home for me to sneak out. You're never here, and it gets really old, really fast, sitting around every afternoon by myself. For all you would know, maybe I do stuff like this all the time."

I know I'm going too far and I should stop. But I can't. Mom thinks I don't have my own voice? Well, maybe it's time she heard me, loud and clear. I grab the application for Camp Colonial and crumple it up. "And I am not going to some stupid pre-high-school camp just because you want me to. And you want to know why? Because I don't want to go to law school and become a lawyer— just so I can work all the time and never see my family. Because the last thing in the world I'd ever want to be—is anything like you."

After I finish, I expect Mom to yell at me or tell me to go to my room, but she doesn't do either of those things. She doesn't *do* anything. She just stands there, drilling me with her ice-blue eyes, unblinking. Unmoved.

"Pull yourself together," Mom says finally. "You can speak to your father when he gets home."

Then she turns around and leaves. And she doesn't look back.

The long and short of it is this: I'm grounded until my parents feel like they can trust me again. Or until the day

I die, whichever comes first. I can still go to Winston's dress rehearsal and Groove It Up on Saturday, but starting next week I'll have to go straight home after school and call Mom—from our home phone—as soon as I get there. And if something like this ever happens again, they said they would actually hire an after-school babysitter.

After Dad came home, he walked into my room and told me we needed a family meeting so we could all talk. Dad spent about ten minutes trying to get Mom and me to "open up and share our feelings," before he finally gave up and handed down my punishment. Besides being grounded and threatened with a babysitter, I had to give him my cell phone and my laptop.

"You're to have no online or phone access, period." Then Dad asked me if I've ever sneaked out of the house before.

"I told Mom earlier, it's not sneaking out if—"

Dad held up a hand. "I think you know what I'm asking. And I want an answer."

"No," I said. "Never."

The whole time Mom never spoke. In fact, she wouldn't even look at me. Later, after she'd gone upstairs, I tried to reason with Dad and get him to lessen my punishment.

"Don't you think you guys are overreacting?" I said.

"No, actually," Dad answered. "You broke the rules. And just as important, you upset your mother."

"No I didn't. She was a total ice queen. It was like she didn't even hear me."

But I heard something later that night when I was on my way to the kitchen to get a snack. Strangled, gurgling sounds were leaking from Mom's office. She'd left the door cracked open. I peeked in and saw her shoulders shake as she quietly sobbed into her hands. I guess Mom isn't such an ice queen, after all.

I thought about saying something to her, telling her I hadn't meant the horrible things I'd said. But then I remembered the last time I'd eavesdropped on Mom, when she told Principal Allen I was too much of a follower to be the PlanMaster. So I tiptoed away and went downstairs.

And I tried not to care that she was crying.

Chapter 15

☆ ☆ ☆

True Confession: When you're popular, it feels like people always want to be near you. But that doesn't mean they know you.

Crowds are usually not a problem for me. People tend to get out of the way when anyone from the Court walks down the hallway. Kristy—whose family goes to church—says it's like Moses parting the Red Sea. So the next morning I can tell something's wrong as soon as I set foot on campus.

No one moves as I walk down the hall. Most people are too busy staring at me—and not in a good way. One girl deliberately smacks into my shoulder as we pass each other, and I drop my history textbook on my foot.

"Ouch!"

"Poor Plastic Polly, did you hurt yourself?" calls another

girl as I bend down to pick up the textbook. Weirder than the fact that someone's calling me Plastic Polly to my face is that several students are smiling, like they think it's funny.

What's going on? I think as I silently hurry away. Did I accidentally walk into the wrong school today?

Someone taped a note to my locker, and I smile for the first time this morning as I rip it off and start spinning the combination lock.

I've unloaded and reloaded my backpack and am just about to open the note when I hear Alyssa's voice behind me. "Are you okay?"

"Not really," I grumble, turning around. "I'm grounded until I'm at least thirty, my parents hate me, and for some reason everyone is acting totally weird today."

Alyssa's eyes go wide. "So you don't know? Didn't you get my voice mails?"

"Know what? And no, I didn't get them, because my parents took away my phone."

"Why are you grounded?" Not waiting for an answer, Alyssa adds, "Polly, everyone's talking about you—it's all over school."

"What's all over school?" I open the note, but before I can look at it, Alyssa places a hand on my shoulder.

"Everyone's saying you've been hanging out with

American River's PlanMaster, and that you're actually trying to help them win."

"What?" I glance down at the note. The word "TRAITOR" is written in big block letters across the top. Below that is a drawing of a boy and a girl holding hands. Both of them have the word "PlanMaster" written across their shirts.

"Everyone was talking about it online last night," Alyssa says. "A friend of a friend of a friend messaged me and everyone else in the choir saying that Melinda saw you and the American River PlanMaster holding hands at Chip's yesterday."

"We weren't holding hands." I can feel my face flushing. "We were just—shaking hands."

"Are you saying it's true?" Alyssa looks shocked. "You've been hanging out with him?"

"No. I mean, yes—but just that one time. Look, it's complicated, okay?" I close my eyes, trying to think this through. So yesterday Melinda texted not only Mrs. Huff, but several other people as well. And if Alyssa—who, social-status-wise, is about as far away from Melinda and the Court as you can get—knows I was hanging out with Justin yesterday, then everyone else at school probably knows too.

When I open my eyes, Alyssa is staring at me. "I was messaging and texting people all night sticking up for you—telling them there's no way you would do something like that and that Melinda is a liar."

"I know it looks really bad," I tell Alyssa, "but I swear I'm not helping American River. Justin's just been trying to apologize since that night at the mall when—"

"What?" Alyssa takes a step backward. "What are you talking about? You *just said* you only hung out with him once. Now you're saying it's more than once? Are you completely incapable of telling the truth?"

"Alyssa." I grab her arm before she has a chance to walk away from me. "I promise I'm not helping their team. If anything, it's our team that needs help."

"Melinda is also saying she overheard you telling Justin all about our acts."

"I didn't, I swear. Yes, I saw Justin yesterday, but I didn't tell him anything about our Talent Team. Melinda is lying."

Alyssa stares at me steadily. "Even if I believe you, no one else will."

As the morning progresses from one painful class to another, I can tell Alyssa is right. No one will believe me. Not that anyone *asks* me if the rumors are true. Nope, I get lots of dirty looks, and conversations stop when I pass by, but no one actually speaks to me. Except for Kate Newport in history class, when she informs me—in a voice loud enough so everyone hears—I should start doing my own homework, and that, by the way, she'd like all her jewelry back. In that same class when I ask Kristy if I can borrow a pencil, she ignores me, so I don't take any notes on Mrs. Davenport's lecture on the fall of the Roman Empire. Which earns me a second lecture from Mrs. Davenport—this one on the importance of taking my education seriously. Then she assigns me an extra essay to write on the political system in ancient Rome.

Every single person in the entire school seems to know that I was at Chip's yesterday. Bethany Perkins even managed to slip an article about me and Justin into today's issue of the *Winston Times* titled "Did PlanMaster Polly Just Shatter Winston's Chances?" There's a picture of me on the cover, right next to a picture of Shattered Stars, and the article says that if the rumors are true, then Winston can just forget about the concert and the TV spot on *Good Morning, Maple Oaks*. Right after I finish reading the article, I get called out of class and spend twenty minutes explaining the whole situation to Principal Allen and Mr. Fish. Both of them tell me they believe me, but are still disappointed in my lack of discretion.

Three more nasty notes arrive in my locker. And after fourth period, when I'm hiding in a bathroom stall, trying to quietly give myself a private pep talk, two girls enter the restroom and start gossiping about me.

"But," the first girl finishes up, "I heard Polly is saying it's not true."

"Right," the second girl scoffs. "Like you can trust anything Plastic Polly says."

At lunch after I've gone through the cafeteria line, I stand holding my tray, wondering for the first time in over a year if I'm allowed to sit at the Court. Melinda is still sitting at the head of the table, and Jenna is still sitting next to her. Next to Jenna is Kate Newport. Everyone, from Lindsey, to Derek, to Kristy and the rest of the cheerleaders are staring intently at Kate while she speaks. Two guesses who they're talking about.

I end up tossing my lunch into the trash. Maybe I'll hang out with Alyssa again instead. But at the top of the staircase leading to the Dungeon I pause. Would Alyssa eat lunch with me? Would *anyone* in Winston Academy eat lunch with me today?

Finally I turn around and head for the library. With the dress rehearsal this afternoon and Groove It Up tomorrow, I might as well get a head start on Mrs. Davenport's essay now.

In sixth period English class Derek is lounging in my seat next to Melinda, so I have to sit in the back of the class. Which actually isn't so bad. As one student after another stands up to give their book report, I relax for the first time all day. Since I'm sitting in the back, people seem to have forgotten about me.

"Okay and next up is . . ." Mr. Fish checks his list. "Polly Pierce. She'll be presenting on *Little Women*."

Everyone turns, and thirty pairs of hostile eyes glare at me. Butterflies flutter in my stomach as I pick up my notes, walk to the front of the class, and face everyone.

For a minute I wonder if, instead of giving my book report, I should explain that I wasn't helping American River. If I told everyone that this is all just a big misunderstanding, would they believe me?

Probably not. After all, you can't trust anything Plastic Polly says, right?

"Whenever you're ready," Mr. Fish prompts.

I look down at my notes. I had my presentation all ready to go. I had planned to gush on and on about how Jo March was my favorite character, even though that's not actually true. Jo is the character everyone likes best, and really, saying she's your favorite is the cool answer.

But standing up here, I realize I'm wearing clothes I bought to please other people, I'm about to speak in a voice I've practiced to please other people, and I'm ready to give a fake answer to please other people.

And you know what? I'm sick of it.

So instead, I tell the class the truth. I tell them how, in my opinion, *Little Women* is a book about girls trying to figure out who they are and what they want in life. And that I know most people like the character of Jo the best, because she's the confident tomboy who doesn't care what anyone thinks, while everyone believes her younger sister Amy—who is *my* favorite character—is a spoiled brat, just because she cares about her looks and got to go to Europe with her aunt, and Jo didn't.

But why would anyone want to be Jo? She doesn't care about clothes, or boys, or parties, and she likes to spend hours alone in her room writing. How boring is *that*? Being alone in your house isn't that great, I tell the class. And it's not Amy's fault she got picked to go to Europe. She was in the right place at the right time, and when an opportunity was handed to her, she was smart enough to take it. She got to travel, and do fun things, and flirt with a cute boy. Why does that make her a brat? Especially if, in the end, she figured out who she wanted to be?

When I'm finished, I return to my seat. In the row in front of me I hear one girl whisper to another, "Figures. Plastic Polly *would* like Amy the best."

But I don't let it shake me. For once I gave a real, true answer. And if someone doesn't like it, too bad for them.

Chapter 16

☆ ☆ ☆

True Confession: I still have my stuffed teddy bear that I named Amelia Earhart, but whenever any of the Court girls come over, I hide her in my closet.

WHEN I RETURN HOME AFTER THE GROOVE IT UP DRESS rehearsal, which did *not* go well, I immediately notice two things. One, both my parents are already home from work. And two, Mom is making dinner tonight. I don't mean she's scooping food out of a take-out container and plopping it onto a plate. I mean she's actually cooking dinner. The oven is turned on and everything. I can tell because whatever's in there smells like it's starting to burn.

"Go wash up," Mom says. "Tonight we're having a family dinner. All three of us."

"Okay." I slink into my bedroom, lie down on my bed,

and hug Amelia Earhart to my chest. The dress rehearsal was sort of a disaster. While the Talent Team rehearsed, the planning committee ignored me and spent the whole time huddled together, whispering.

Finally I was able to pull Lindsey aside and explain that I wasn't helping the American River team.

"I don't know, Polly," Lindsey said. "It doesn't look good. First you fire Melinda and Jenna. Then Melinda says she saw you with Justin yesterday. And now at lunch Kate told us you and Alyssa formed your own judging club and that she was expected to just agree with whatever you two wanted."

"Kate said that?"

Lindsey nodded. "Is it true?"

I didn't know how to answer that. *Was* it true? It was true that Alyssa and I—when it came to judging, anyway— had similar tastes. But had we done the same thing to Kate that Melinda and Jenna had done to me?

I pulled Kate aside to try to talk to her, but she just shrugged and said, "Melinda invited me to the Court." I realized Kate didn't particularly care if the rumors about me and Justin were true. She was just happy she'd finally gotten her invite, something I could've given her at any time but hadn't.

"I'm so sorry, Kate," I said, and hoped she knew I meant for more than just the mess with Justin.

In the dining room Mom, Dad, and I sip mineral water and stare at the lit candles and the decorative squashes Mom placed in the center of the table. No one moves to try the food.

Mom made a pan of corn bread and a pot of chili. The corn bread is looking decidedly charred, so no one has scooped a piece out yet. And the chili—well, I've never seen chili with a greenish tinge to it.

Mom serves Dad and me a heaping bowl of chili. "Dig in!" she says eagerly, taking a sip of mineral water.

"Aren't you going to have any?" Dad looks at the empty bowl in front of Mom.

"Oh, no." Mom waves a hand. "I snacked while I was cooking. I'm absolutely stuffed."

Dad looks at me as if to say, *You first!* but I shake my head slightly and point at him.

Dad grabs Mom's fingers and kisses the back of her hand. "Looks wonderful, Laura." Then he raises a spoonful of chili. "Bon appétit!" He chews for about five seconds, then starts to cough violently. "Water!" he gasps.

Mom grabs the pitcher and refills his glass. Dad chugs it down quickly. "More." After another glass of hastily gulped water, he says, "I'm all right. My allergies must be acting up." Then, in a casual voice, he says, "Laura, how much salt did you put in this?"

Mom shrugs. "The recipe got wet from some water on the counter. I think it said two T something. So I put in two tablespoons."

I quickly put my spoon down. "Mom, I think it was supposed to be two teaspoons."

"Oh." Mom's smile fades.

"But that's fine," Dad says quickly. "Measurements don't matter." He looks pointedly at my spoon and gives me a look that clearly tells me I'd better start eating, *now*.

I pick my spoon back up and sprinkle a thick layer of shredded cheese over my chili and top it off with about two cups of sour cream. Then I take a bite. I don't think I've ever tasted chili like this before. I can't detect any meat or beans in it. Maybe it's supposed to be vegetable chili?

"Eat up," Mom says. "There's dessert in the fridge when we're done."

Dad and I glance at each other. I can't help but wonder if aliens kidnapped my mother while I was at school and left a Martha Stewart wannabe in her place.

"How was the dress rehearsal?" Mom asks in a bright voice. "Do you feel ready for Groove It Up tomorrow?"

"Yeah, it was okay," I say, even though it was most definitely not okay. I take my knife and attempt to cut out a piece of cornbread. The bottom is burnt to the pan, so I settle for scooping out crispy chunks and dumping them onto my napkin.

"What about school?" Mom asks. "How was your day today?"

I don't feel like telling Mom that today was the worst day I've ever had in middle school, so instead I answer, "Okay."

"Okay," Mom echoes. "Fabulous." She takes a long swig of water.

From the living room we hear Dad's cell phone ring. He starts to get up—looking way too happy to have a reason to leave—when Mom stops him.

"Sit down. Whatever it is can wait until we're finished. We're having a nice family dinner, like the nice, happy family we are," she says through gritted teeth. Then she turns back to me. "Didn't you tell me you had an English presentation today? How did that go?"

I shrug. "It went fine."

"So everything in your life is either okay or fine?" Mom asks. "What about the chili, is that okay too? Or do you have a more definitive opinion on that subject?"

"Laura," Dad begins, "I don't think—"

"Forget it," Mom says, waving her hand. "What about Kelsey, how is she doing?"

"How would I know how Kelsey is doing?" I say. "You took away my phone, remember?"

Mom bunches up her napkin and tosses it onto the table. "So I'm not supposed to ask you questions about your life, is that it? Because I thought this was what you wanted, a nice family dinner every night, with a mother who isn't such an absentee screwup?"

"I never said that. And what about what you want?" I say, my voice rising. "Don't you want a daughter who isn't such a follower? 'Oh, Principal Allen,'" I mimic Mom's voice, "'I'm sorry, but my daughter's too much of a follower to be the PlanMaster. She's too busy shopping and texting to lead anything.'"

Mom turns white. "Polly, I'm so sorry. I never meant—"

"Forget it." I scoot my chair back and stand up. "I'm going upstairs. I'm not hungry anymore."

I stomp up to my room, slam the door, and flop down onto my bed. I get what Mom's trying to do, but it feels totally unfair. Yesterday she flipped out because I forgot to tell her where I was going, and she wouldn't even listen to me explain what happened. And now today she thinks she can come home, cook one lousy meal (and I do mean *lousy*), and all of a sudden we're supposed to be best friends? I don't think so.

After staring at the ceiling for several minutes, I grab *The PlanMaster's PlanMaster* off my nightstand. I want to run through it one last time, just to make sure I've got everything covered. But the words just seem to blend together, so finally I put it aside.

There's a soft knock, and Mom pushes the door open. She sits down next to me. She's holding the crumpled application for Camp Colonial. "I'm sorry you overheard that," she says softly. "I don't think you're a follower."

"Then why did you say it?"

"I don't know. I guess . . . I guess I want to make sure you walk your own path in life, instead of following someone else's."

I tap the application with my finger. "That's not my path. And maybe you knew what you wanted to do, and who you wanted to be, when you were my age, but I don't. I don't know what I like to do, or what I'm good at, or even if I'm good at anything."

"Well," Mom says, "I think you're good at a lot of things. You're certainly a much better cook than I am."

"Yeah, that's true."

Mom smiles faintly and sighs. "Would you rather have a mom who bakes and scrapbooks and does all those kinds of . . . I don't know, *mom* things?"

I don't answer right away, because the truth is that sometimes I wish she didn't work so much. But Mom is passionate and smart, and every day she shows me it's possible to have a dream, go after it, and make it come true.

"No, I guess not," I answer. "But what about you? Do you wish you had a daughter who was more of a leader? A daughter who was dead set on becoming a lawyer?"

"No, I guess not," Mom says. Then she picks up the camp application and tears it to shreds. I know it costs her something to do that.

Mom holds up her cell phone so I can see it. "See this app right here? It's an online organization system. Maybe when you get your phone back, we can download it for you and I can show you how to use it. You've been doing such a great job as the PlanMaster."

I thank Mom and tell her that anytime she's willing to give me back my phone, I would love to look at the app with her.

I hear a gurgling sound, and it takes me a second to realize it's coming from Mom's stomach.

"Hungry?" I ask.

"Starving."

"I thought you weren't hungry because you snacked before dinner?"

"Well . . . I sampled some of the chili . . ." Mom makes a yuck face.

"Want me to help you cook something else for dinner?"

Mom breathes a huge sigh of relief. "I thought you'd never ask. Also, I think we'll have to throw out the dessert I made." We laugh as we stand up and head for the kitchen.

Look, some mothers like to make homemade dinners and volunteer for the PTA. My mother likes to download organization apps for my cell phone. And you know what? I wouldn't change her, even if I could.

Chapter 17

☆ ☆ ☆

*True Confession: I never got rid of my old best
friend's necklace. Just in case.*

SOMETHING'S NOT RIGHT.

Four hours before Groove It Up starts, I'm sitting in Winston's auditorium, wearing my pink glittery T-shirt and checking my watch for the hundredth
time. Why isn't anyone here yet? I've been waiting for
an hour already, but no one from the planning committee has showed up.

I stare at my long to-do list and fight the gnawing
feeling in my chest that something is really, *really* wrong.
Last night I was pretty clear at the dress rehearsal what
time I needed the planning committee to arrive. I even

announced it over the loudspeaker. I had to, since no one would actually speak to me.

I'm rifling through the bag of T-shirts from Zack's, double-checking that I have enough for everyone, when I hear the double doors open behind me. I turn around, expecting to see someone from the planning committee. Instead, I see Kelsey.

"They're not coming." Kelsey crosses the room and drops into the seat next to me.

"Who's not coming?"

"The planning committee."

"Very funny." But when Kelsey doesn't smile I add, "Seriously? *None* of them are coming?"

"They're boycotting," Kelsey says matter-of-factly. "Everyone except Kristy."

"They wouldn't. They want to win the prizes."

Kelsey shrugs. "Melinda says you've shut them out anyway, so what's the difference? Mrs. Huff is even writing a letter to Principal Allen protesting your behavior as the PlanMaster."

"*My* behavior? Great." I'd like to talk to Mrs. Huff about her and Jenna's behavior, but any anger I might feel is quickly replaced by panic. Jenna and Mrs. Huff were in charge of the bake sale during intermission. Melinda was supposed to help the Talent Team get ready. Lindsey was supposed to—

"This is the part where you don't freak out," Kelsey says.

"*Don't* freak out? Are you crazy? Do you have any idea—"

"I know," Kelsey says, as calm as ever, "but we'll figure something out."

"Right." I lean my head back against the chair and start taking deep breaths, just like I've seen Mom do when she gets super stressed. "By the way, I'm pretty sure after this is over I'll be banished from the Court. I don't think even you can stop that. You should leave right now, before you become unpopular by association."

Kelsey looks down. With her good hand she traces her finger over a picture Molly drew on her cast—of a queen sitting on her throne. "Want to know something? It was kind of a relief, being out of school the past few weeks. I mean, I wanted to be the PlanMaster, but"—Kelsey shrugs helplessly—"details aren't really my thing. And I figured Melinda would find a way to blame me if we lost."

"We *are* going to lose. So you should leave." I close my eyes. "You can blame everything on me. Then next week you can come back to school and banish me yourself."

"Hmmm . . . tempting." Kelsey nudges me with her shoulder. "But I'll take option B: We win. Then next week we'll rub Melinda's smug little nose in it." Kelsey picks up the bag of T-shirts from Zack's. "Any chance you have a shirt in there for me, Madame PlanMaster?"

The doors whoosh open again. Alyssa walks in, and Kelsey falls silent. I can hear the electric hum of the overhead lights as Kelsey and I stare at her.

"I didn't think you were coming today," I say.

"I almost didn't." And from the way she glances at Kelsey, it looks like Alyssa wishes she *hadn't* come. "Tasha overheard Melinda and Jenna talking about boycotting. She thought they were kidding, but I thought I should see if you needed help . . ." Alyssa trails off and glances again at Kelsey.

Which is when I realize that this is the first time since that day in the cafeteria that the three of us have been alone in the same room together. Talking.

Kelsey crosses her arms and glares at Alyssa.

"What are you staring at?" Alyssa asks.

"You," Kelsey answers. "You've been hanging out with Polly, and you still haven't apologized."

"Kelsey," I say. "Come on, let's—"

"Me?" Alyssa says. "*You're* the ones who should be apologizing."

"For what?" Kelsey stands up. "You're the one who's been calling us names behind our backs. That's not cool, Alyssa, and you know it. You don't do that to your friends."

"Oh yeah?" Alyssa says in a shrill voice. "Well, even if I wanted to apologize, how could I? I'm not allowed to eat at the Court, remember? And you two always walk around like you think you're all that and pretend like I'm invisible. And you're always surrounded by your little entourage."

"Would you two please just *stop*?"

Alyssa ignores me. "Both of you ditched me just so you could eat at a stupid lunch table. You chose popularity over your friends."

Kelsey shrugs. "And you chose *not* being popular over your friends."

Alyssa rolls her eyes at Kelsey and turns like she's going to leave.

"Wait, Alyssa, don't go. Can't the two of you stop being so stubborn just for one second?" Not for the first time, I wonder what the past year would have been like if one of us had just said we were sorry. "Look, are either of you mad at me right now?"

"No," Kelsey says.

"Not really," Alyssa answers.

"Then can't you call a temporary truce just for a minute? Groove It Up is in just a few hours, and it's going to be a disaster."

"It's *not* going to be a disaster," Kelsey says.

"Yeah . . . it might come close, though," Alyssa says. Then, after Kelsey glares at her, Alyssa adds, "I'm just kidding."

The three of us are silent. Until Kelsey says, "Well, I guess I do walk around like I think I'm all that." She pauses and grins. "Can you blame me, though? I'm Queen Kelsey."

Alyssa bites her lip to keep from smiling. But then she turns serious. "I never spread those nicknames around. I mean, I said them, just once, to someone when I was mad."

Kelsey and I glance at each other. "Who?" I ask.

"Jenna Huff. She thought the nicknames were brilliant."

"I'll just *bet* she did," Kelsey says.

Alyssa and Kelsey are two of the most complicated and stubborn girls I've ever met, and I know this is the closest either of them will ever come to saying they're sorry. But I also know it isn't enough.

"Alyssa," I say, "I'm sorry for ignoring you. You're my best friend—one of my two best friends," I add with a quick glance at Kelsey. "And I miss you. I miss the three of us together."

Alyssa and Kelsey look at each other. Then Alyssa says, "Peacemaker Polly?"

Kelsey sniffs. "Perfect Polly?"

"How about just Polly?" I say.

"Deal." Kelsey tosses Alyssa a T-shirt. "Looks like we've got a lot of work to do."

And with that, we begin picking up the pieces of a broken talent competition.

The three of us spend the next half hour setting up the auditorium. We've moved the ticket and refreshment tables into place in the foyer, and Alyssa has just finished signing Kelsey's cast when Mr. Fish arrives. His expression becomes increasingly annoyed as I tell him about the boycott.

"May I borrow your cell phone?" he asks when I've finished.

"I don't have it right now," I tell him. "You don't have one?"

"No, Miss Pierce, I don't. I think they're a supreme waste of time."

Mr. Fish borrows Kelsey's phone. He calls Mrs. Fish and asks her to bring their daughters early so they can help set up. After he's finished, Alyssa calls some of her drama and choir friends to come and help her and Mr. Fish with the sound and lighting. Then I call Mom, asking her if she can bring snacks for the bake sale.

"You want *me* to bake snacks for you?"

"No, there's not enough time for that. Can you run to the store and pick up some brownies and cookies and stuff?"

"Oh, sure." Relief floods Mom's voice. "*That* I can do."

American River's planning committee arrives. Montana leads the way, and her beady black eyes take in the red-and-yellow Winston banners posted on the left wall. "Playing favorites?" she says, and sneers. "Both schools should be equally represented. Otherwise it's not fair."

"Who is this strange person?" Kelsey whispers loudly.

I shush Kelsey and say, "Turn around, Montana."

Montana eyes the blue American River banners hanging on the right wall. Then she checks Winston's side again—I think to make sure each school has the same amount. "Fine," she concedes, and heads backstage, calling over her shoulder, "I left all of our props and costumes in the dressing room. If I find anything out of place, I'm holding you responsible."

The rest of American River's planning committee—all of them wearing their black polo shirts and khaki pants—

quietly follow after her. Justin brings up the rear and stops in front of me, looking sheepish.

"Mr. Pritchard called me into his office yesterday afternoon, wanting to know if we've been working together. Someone told him they saw us at the diner."

"Even Mr. Pritchard knows?"

"I guess. And somehow Montana found out. Now she thinks I'm trying to help you guys win." Justin looks away, over to the stage, where Zack the emcee is testing out the microphone. "She thinks I have a crush on you."

"Oh? Oh, really?" My voice comes out squeaky.

"Yeah, well . . . So maybe after this is over, do you think I could call you?"

I shake my head. "I wish. I'm currently grounded, and phoneless. But are you going to Maple Oaks High next year?" After Justin nods I say, "Me too. See you there?"

Justin smiles. "See you there." He turns to walk away. "But I'm still going to win today."

"Dream on," I call.

"You dream on," Justin says before he disappears backstage. "You have no idea what we're planning."

I don't have time to think about whatever American River has planned, because both school's Talent Teams arrive, and chaos ensues. Backstage I placed a line of duct tape on the floor, dividing the space into two equal sections. Justin directs his team stage right to the American River section, while I herd my team stage left to the Winston Academy section.

After that I spend ten minutes helping Tasha and Dominique locate their costumes, which seem to have suddenly gone missing. Mr. Fish's daughters arrive, and I assign the three oldest to the ticket and refreshment tables. Then I help Justin separate Kristy and the captain of the American River cheerleading squad, who get into a name-calling match.

"Thanks for not boycotting with Melinda and Jenna," I say to Kristy as we walk back to the Winston section.

"Melinda and Jenna need to get a grip," Kristy says with a furious look at American River's cheerleaders. She glances over at Justin. "So he's their PlanMaster? He's cute, in a dorky sort of way."

"Yeah, I guess. But I promise, I wasn't—"

Kristy waves her hand. "Whatever. I think I believe you. And either way, I'm gonna wipe the floor with their cheerleaders."

"That's the spirit." We high-five, and Kristy goes back to her girls.

Mom arrives with brownies, cookies, and several pies she picked up from Chip's.

"Great." I make a check on my clipboard. "Can you unload them in the foyer?"

Mom looks around at people scurrying left and right. "Polly, I just wanted to tell you—"

"Can it wait?" I ask, noticing that Kelsey has mistaken Betsy the gymnast for a younger student and is trying to shoo her from backstage.

"Kelsey!" I bellow. "Stop messing with my Talent Team!" Then to no one in particular I yell, "Where's the program with all the acts listed? Kelsey clearly needs one!"

"Didn't you tell me Melinda was supposed to pick them up from the printer?" Alyssa comes up behind me.

I look down at my clipboard. "Shoot!"

"Where are they?" Mom asks. "I can pick them up."

After I tell Mom the name of the printer, she reaches into her pocket and pulls out my cell phone. "Just in case I need to get ahold of you." I reach for my phone, but Mom moves it out of my grasp. "However, after this is over, it's going right back into my purse. Okay?"

"Okay. Thanks." I slip my phone into my pocket. When Mom doesn't leave, I ask, "Anything else?"

Mom fidgets with the strap on her purse. "I wanted to tell you that—"

"Would Alyssa Grace and PlanMaster Polly Pierce please report to the

sound booth?" booms Mr. Fish's voice over the sound system.

"Can we talk later, Mom?" I say, and hurry away.

Alyssa and I spend the next several minutes helping Mr. Fish and a couple of Alyssa's friends hunt through about a hundred CDs for the Soccer Shakers' karaoke music.

"This would've been a lot easier if they hadn't brought their entire music collection," Alyssa grumbles.

After we finish, I find Kelsey. "How are things going backstage?"

"Great." Kelsey nods. "All eight acts are almost ready to go."

I know there's something not right about what she's saying, but I can't figure out what. I don't have time to think about it, though, because Kai and Aidan come rushing up to tell me that Montana's guarding the door to the dressing room, preventing them from getting their hacky sacks.

"She won't let anyone from Winston inside because she's stored American River's props there and she's afraid we'll mess them up," Kai says.

"Wait!" I call to Kelsey, who's started to walk away. "There's someone on American River's planning committee who thinks our dressing room is her own personal property. Go set her straight."

"You got it." Kelsey takes off.

Then one of the Soccer Shakers, a boy named Aaron, stops me. "I can't find my uniform shirt! We're supposed to wear them for our act!"

"So go get a shirt from one of your friends. We're starting pretty soon, and I saw half the soccer team sitting in the audience. They're wearing their uniforms." I check my clipboard again. Something doesn't seem right. Am I forgetting something?

"Yeah, but it won't have my number on it," Aaron whines. "I want people to see *my* number."

I hug my clipboard to my hip and sigh. "Do you want to hear just how much I *don't care* about your number right now? Go out there. Go get your friend's shirt. Or so *help* me, I will sic Kelsey on you."

"You called?" Kelsey emerges from backstage. She's followed by a slightly terrified and clearly contrite-looking Montana.

"No, we're good." I look pointedly at Aaron. "Now go out there and get that shirt."

"Five minutes, everyone! Five minutes!" Mr. Fish calls out.

Mom arrives with the programs and hands me one. She leaves to pass the rest out to the audience. She's followed by Mr. Pritchard, who's grumbling that things would've been going a lot smoother if American River had hosted Groove It Up.

The overhead lights flicker on and off, signaling that the show's about to start. I close my eyes. Backstage smells like a mixture of sweat, too much perfume, and anticipation. I hear Winston's Talent Team excitedly wishing each other good luck and Mr. Fish giving Zack some last-minute instructions. For the first time all day, I breathe a long sigh of relief. Even with the boycott, things are coming together, and it looks like everything's going to be okay.

But when I open my program and scan the list of acts, I freeze. The unease I felt earlier comes flooding back. "Kelsey!" I hiss. "Can you come over here?"

"What?" Kelsey raises her cast like it's a hot-pink baseball bat. "Need me to beat anyone up?"

"No. What did you mean when you said all *eight* acts were ready?"

Kelsey shrugs. "I tracked them down and made sure everyone has everything they need." She taps the program. "Would've been easier if I'd had that, though."

Over the sound system, Zack's voice booms, *"Laaaadiiiees and Geeennntlemen! Welcome to the fortieth annual Groove It Up talent show competition. I'm your host, Zack Wilson!"*

Applause as loud as a fall thunderstorm bursts from the audience, and I have to shout at Kelsey, "They changed it this year! We've got *ten* acts!" I shove the program at her.

"That would have been helpful to know a lot earlier!" Kelsey shouts back.

"I'm proud to introduce this year's judges: Superintendent Nichols! Principal Martinez from Maple Oaks High School! Annnnnd . . . our very own . . . Mayor Peterson!"

Kelsey reads the program, and I shout, "Who *haven't* you seen today?"

Kelsey looks up. "Derek Tanner and the Glitter Girls!"

"And finally, may I have this year's PlanMasters, Polly Pierce and Justin Goodwin!"

"Find out where they are!" I shout before stepping onto the stage.

Chapter 18

☆ ☆ ☆

*True Confession: Sometimes when I'm alone in my room,
I lip-sync to the radio and pretend I'm a rock star.*

I'M GREETED WITH CHEERS AND BOOS FROM THE AUDI-
ence as I take my place next to Justin on the stage. The fami-
lies from Winston Academy are sitting on the left, most of
them dressed in red and yellow. On the right, people hold
signs saying, AMERICAN RIVER IS A WINNER! On Winston's
side I see Principal Allen sitting in the front row, right next
to my parents. Flashes of white light twinkle like shooting
stars as Zack poses for pictures with the judges.

While I wait, I step back a couple paces and glance
backstage. Kelsey is standing in the wings, talking on her
cell phone.

Please, please, please let Derek and the Glitter Girls be here, I think, trying not to panic. Because I have no idea what I'm going to do if we're short two acts.

Once the pictures are finished, Zack moves to center stage. "We've got a great show planned for you tonight! To celebrate our fortieth anniversary, tonight's winning school will receive some fabulous prizes! The winning Talent Team will appear next week on *Good Morning, Maple Oaks*, and the entire school will receive a private concert with our favorite hometown band, Shattered Stars!" More applause, so loud I see a couple people clamp their hands over their ears. Finally Zack motions for everyone to be quiet and says, "Dim the lights, please!" A spotlight switches on, and Zack instructs everyone on the stage to form a circle. The audience quiets down, and everything is silent except for the clicking of several camera shutters. "And now, to kick things off, we'll toss a coin to determine which school will have the honor of opening the show. May I have the coin?"

Mr. Pritchard reaches into his pocket, but Mr. Fish stops him. "I've got one." Mr. Fish produces a penny so shiny, it practically glows. "Just picked it up from the bank this morning. If you don't mind."

He reaches past Mr. Pritchard and hands the coin to Zack, who looks at Justin and me. "PlanMasters, call it!"

Justin nods at me.

"I call heads!" I say, hoping I look like I really want to win the toss. But right now I'm trying to remember our program. The Glitter Girls were toward the end, I think. But wasn't Derek one of our first acts?

"All right. HERE. WE. GO!" Zack tosses the penny high into the air, and it spins and twists, a copper star twinkling in the spotlight, until it drops into the center of our circle.

"It's tails!" shouts the mayor.

Cheers erupt from American River's side and boos from Winston Academy's side.

"Will the judges, teacher advisers, and PlanMasters each confirm this is tails?" Zack says.

One by one we each certify it's tails.

"Then I declare this year's annual Groove It Up has now begun!"

More applause from the audience, and everyone hurries off the stage. Alyssa is waiting for me in the wings. "Kelsey told me a couple of the acts are missing. What's going on?"

I shake my head. "Where did Kelsey go?"

"She's on the phone, trying to get ahold of Derek. She can't find him."

"Great." I watch the stage as American River's first act begins. It's a boy and girl tap dancing duo.

"All right," Kelsey says, walking up behind Alyssa. "Here's the scoop: Derek and the Glitter Girls aren't coming."

"They're not coming?" I repeat numbly. "Why?"

"They're boycotting too."

"You're kidding."

"Boycotting?" Alyssa snorts. "Give me a break. Derek probably just ran out of eggs. And Jenna's friends are terrible dancers."

Kelsey shoots her a look.

"What?" Alyssa says. "It's true. We're better off without them."

"We're not better off without them." For the first time, I'm sorry I've memorized most of *The PlanMaster's PlanMaster*. "The rules say we'll be automatically disqualified if we can't produce the required amount of acts. When is Derek supposed to go on?"

Kelsey opens her program. "He's second. And the Glitter Girls were the final act."

The tap dancers finish, and Zack's voice booms over the sound system, *"And first up for Winston Academy . . . the Soccer Shakers!"*

Kelsey and Alyssa look at me like they expect me to make some kind of decision. But I have no idea what to do. So I ignore them and watch while the Soccer Shakers take the stage and begin their impersonation of a boy band. I peek out the side of the curtain. I expect the audience to cringe, but a lot of people—including my parents and all three of the judges—are laughing. The Soccer Shakers are so bad, they're actually hysterical.

Alyssa places a hand on my shoulder. "Polly, it's going to be okay. Things like this happen all the time in drama and choir. Stuff comes up at the last minute, and you just have to deal with it." She pauses and adds, "We'll think of something."

Which, actually, does make me think of something.

I turn to Alyssa. "I need you."

"What do you mean?"

"I need a second act, pronto. Someone who can get up there and blow the crowd away. Please, Alyssa?"

"I don't know, Polly." Alyssa looks unconvinced. "I don't have my music. Or a costume."

"We'll find you a costume. And what do you need music for? Can't you sing without music?"

When she doesn't answer right away, I add, "Please, Alyssa? You wanted a slot on the Talent Team. This is your chance."

Alyssa hesitates. Then she breaks into a wide smile. "All right. I'll do it."

While Alyssa hunts for a costume, I send Kelsey to tell

Zack we've switched our second act. Meanwhile, American River's next act goes on, a mime that, actually, is totally boring.

"Are you ready?" I ask Alyssa, helping her adjust her costume. She found a sparkling blue dress from the drama department.

Alyssa closes her eyes. "Ready."

"Ladies and Gentlemen, I've just been informed there's been a change to Winston Academy's program. Replacing Derek Tanner will be . . . Alyssa Grace."

"Knock 'em dead," I say.

Before Alyssa can respond, Montana stomps over to us. Her beady black eyes look fierce. "I object. You can't just change the program. It's against the rules."

"No, it's not. Go look it up in *The PlanMaster's PlanMaster*. You can change the acts at any time, if needed."

"Yeah, and besides," Alyssa chimes in, "don't you know the first rule of show business? The show must go on."

We giggle and turn away from a still complaining Montana, and Alyssa gives my shoulder a squeeze. "I'm sorry I never called you back last year."

Then Alyssa steps out onto the stage. And she begins to sing. No music. Just Alyssa with the silvery spotlight shining on her. Her voice starts out soft. Wispy, lilting. Like a feather floating on the breeze. From my spot at the edge of the curtain, it looks like the audience is leaning forward, straining to hear her. But slowly Alyssa's voice grows and gains momentum, soaring like the wind itself.

"Wow," breathes a nearby member of American River's planning committee. "She's really good."

"Oh, shut up," Montana hisses, and stomps off.

Standing there, watching Alyssa sing, I forget I'm still one act short. I forget I still have a million other things to do. I forget everything, and everyone. Except Alyssa.

"Was she always this good?" Kelsey comes up behind me.

"She was always good," I say without taking my eyes off Alyssa. "But now she's amazing."

It occurs to me, listening to Alyssa sing, that everyone deserves their chance on the stage. I never would have voted for the Soccer Shakers—I think they're a bunch of goofs. But everyone liked watching them perform. So who am I to judge who has to stand in the shadows and who gets the chance to shine? I look at the audience. I bet there are talents hidden within each one of us. Sometimes it just takes some of us longer to find them than others.

Alyssa finishes on a high note, and the audience is silent. Then Winston's side rises up and gives her a standing ovation. American River's side remains seated, and looks highly annoyed.

"Beautiful," Kelsey whispers. The applause continues, until Zack booms over the sound system that we still have several more acts to go before intermission.

A crowd swarms Alyssa as she walks backstage. I wave to her and mouth, *Congratulations*.

"Okay," Kelsey says. "That's done. So what are we going to do about the final act?"

"I don't know. I'm thinking."

But nothing comes to me as one act and then another performs. During intermission I have Alyssa quietly make a couple of inquiries to see if there's anyone who could go on at the last minute. But after intermission ends, she comes back shaking her head.

"Don't you have any friends who play musical instruments?" I ask as another act from American River begins, a cute boy playing the saxophone.

"Yeah," Alyssa says, "but most of them aren't here. And if they are, it's not like they brought their instruments with them."

As the show goes on, I realize that, surprisingly enough, we're competitive. Tasha and Dominique, the Shakespeare Twins, also get a standing ovation when they rap to *Hamlet*. And the audience seems amazed by Kai and Aidan's hacky sack routine.

I peek over at the judges' table. They seem to be thoroughly enjoying watching Kristy and the cheerleaders perform. The judges don't score each act individually; they announce the winning school after seeing the entire show. And right now I think it could go either way.

After we congratulate Kristy and her girls on a great routine, Kelsey and Alyssa and I fall silent. The sharp panic I felt earlier seems to have settled in my chest and turned stale. This late in the game it'll be next to impossible to find a replacement act.

Zack steps out to center stage. "And for American River's final act, may I present . . . the Rockin' River Choir!"

Kelsey, Alyssa, and I watch as a choir of thirty students files onto the stage and begins to sing. And when two boys appear with electric guitars and the choir starts rocking out with them, the audience goes wild.

Justin is on the other side of the stage, in the wings, fist bumping with the rest of his planning committee. So that was their big act.

Finally Alyssa says, "What should I tell Zack?"

I sigh. "Tell him the truth. Tell him we don't have a final act."

"No," Kelsey says. "We're not giving up. There's got to be something we can do."

"There's not. And we're out of time." I turn to Alyssa. "Go tell him."

American River's choir launches into another song—apparently they're determined to go out with a bang—and I tiptoe away from the curtain, slump down against the wall, and hug my clipboard to my chest. Kelsey joins me, and we lean against each other.

"You did the best you could," she whispers. "Much better than I ever could've done."

I shake my head and don't look at her. Because if I do, I'm afraid the tears I feel building up behind my eyes will come spilling out. In a couple more minutes I'm supposed to produce our closing act. And I've got nothing. I close my eyes and imagine the looks on everyone's faces when Zack announces that Winston Academy doesn't have a final act. Somewhere in the audience I'm sure someone will whisper, "I just *knew* Plastic Polly would screw up the show."

Monday at school I'll probably be banished from the Court. I'll probably be the least popular girl at Winston Academy, but I don't even care anymore. When I told Principal Allen I wanted to be the PlanMaster, I guess I wanted to prove to everyone, to Mom, to Kelsey—and most of all, to myself—that I could be a leader, not just a follower. I wanted them to realize I'm more than Plastic Polly, that there's more to me than what they see on the outside. Now all they'll see is the girl who single-handedly got Winston disqualified from the competition.

"Melinda's going to have a field day with this next week," Kelsey says softly as she watches the American River choir. "I can't believe we're going to lose."

"*You* don't have to lose," I answer in a hollow voice. "On Monday you can just banish me from the Court. We can be, like, *secret* best friends." I look at her and try to smile, but my face muscles won't cooperate. "I know how much you've loved being Queen Kelsey," I add, and she smiles faintly in response.

"Yeah, a lot of times it's pretty great." She looks down and traces Alyssa's signature on her cast. "But . . . sometimes it hasn't been so great, you know? I know I never say it, but . . . I've missed Alyssa too." She rolls her eyes and adds, "Even if she *is* totally stubborn."

Kelsey nudges me with her shoulder. "And secret best friends? Really, Polly? That's the stupidest thing I've ever heard. Besides"—she straightens up and fluffs her hair— "I'm fabulous no matter where I sit in the cafeteria."

Kelsey grins at me, and this time I manage a small smile in return.

Mr. Fish's oldest daughter appears backstage with a plate

of brownies and starts handing them out to everyone. My stomach rumbles when she hands one to me and Kelsey. I take a bite, figuring if I have to lose, at least I have chocolate. The brownies are good. Almost as good as the ones Mrs. Grace used to bake when Kelsey and I would go over to Alyssa's and—

I sit up straight. "Kelsey, do you remember the last time we hung out at Alyssa's house?"

Kelsey looks at me like I just told her two plus two equals red. "You're asking me this *now*?"

"Just think about it. What did we do the last time we hung out at Alyssa's house?"

"How should I know? That was, like, forever ago and—" Kelsey breaks off. I can see her remembering that day, and realizing what I'm about to ask her. "No. No way. You're out of your mind if you think—"

Just then Zack and Alyssa appear backstage. "Polly, what's going on?" Zack says. "Alyssa just told me you don't have a tenth act."

I look at Kelsey. "Please?"

Kelsey sighs and stands up. "All right, fine. But don't say I never did anything for you."

"Great." I whisper to Alyssa the errand I need her to run. I scribble something on my to-do list and show it to Zack. "This is exactly how I want you to announce our final act."

Chapter 19

☆ ☆ ☆

True Confession: I have a recurring nightmare where I walk into a crowded room and everyone holds up a number grading my appearance and how cool they think I am.

KELSEY AND I ARE ALONE ON THE STAGE, WAITING FOR the curtain to rise.

"I'm going to kill you for this," she whispers.

"No, you're not."

"I'll never be able to go out in public ever again."

"Yes, you will. And be quiet. And turn your microphone on."

Kelsey and I both click our microphones on and straighten up at the sound of Zack's voice: "*And now for Winston Academy's final act of the night . . . May I present . . . Plastic Polly and Queen Kelsey: The Karaoke Queens!*"

"You remember how it goes, right?" I whisper to Kelsey out of the side of my mouth.

"Uh, maybe?" Kelsey whispers back. "It's not like we can read the words from the screen this time."

The curtain rises, and the music begins.

I put a hand over my microphone and whisper to Kelsey, "On my count. One, two, three . . . now!"

Kelsey and I both strut to the edge of the stage and launch into our favorite karaoke song, "Celebration."

"Celebrate good times, come on!"

The auditorium isn't darkened. And I really, *really* wish it was. Rows and rows of shocked faces stare back at us. My dad looks ready to cry. One woman on Winston's side actually has a hand clamped over her mouth. Another woman on American River's side comforts her howling toddler and glares at Kelsey and me, like it's our fault her kid is screaming. Which, maybe it is. Have I ever mentioned Kelsey and I have truly terrible voices?

There's a big difference between karaoke-ing in a friend's house and karaoke-ing in a packed auditorium. At Alyssa's house Kelsey and I had a habit of falling down in hysterics, but there's nothing funny about two girls screeching in front of hundreds of people.

Kelsey and I are trying our hardest, but our act is a

disaster. We try to move and shake, but neither of us is a great dancer, and we don't know how to be funny like the Soccer Shakers. I glance over and see Montana peeking out from American River's side of the curtain, an evil grin on her face. On Winston's side Alyssa is wincing as Kelsey and I butcher one note after another.

No one in the audience looks like they're having a good time. A few people from Winston's side stand up and leave. A couple boys on American River's side start booing.

Then suddenly Alyssa runs out onto the stage. At first I think she's come to rescue us and sing the song the way it deserves to be sung, so I hold my microphone out to her. But instead, Alyssa starts making funny faces, doing her crazy chicken hokey pokey dance, and clapping in time to the music. (Which is great, since Kelsey and I were a beat behind.)

In that moment something in the atmosphere changes. The shock seems to fade, and members of the audience, on both sides of the auditorium, start to smile. Someone starts clapping, and soon the whole auditorium joins in. Kelsey and I shrug at each other, and keep singing.

Alyssa is grabbing people by the hand and leading them out onto the stage. First Tasha and Dominique. Then Kai and Aidan. Alyssa jumps down into the audience and leads

Principal Allen to the stage, which makes everyone laugh. Then Kristy and the cheerleaders run out and start dancing.

And that's when I stop thinking about the audience and the humiliation that's sure to follow after this. All I see are my two best friends and that when I really needed them, they've come through for me.

Zack's voice booms over the loudspeakers, *"It would appear that we're ending tonight's show with a dance party! Come on, everyone, and celebrate!"*

I hand my microphone to Tasha. Then I join in with everyone and dance. And I realize I've done it. As many mistakes as I've made these past few weeks, Groove It Up is over, and somehow we've managed to put on a good show. It's taken a while, but I've found my own voice. It may be totally off-key, but at least it's real.

My cell vibrates in my pocket, and I wonder who could possibly be calling me now. I can't help it. I pull out my phone. It's a text from Mom:

I'm so proud of you!

And for the first time in a really long time, I'm proud of myself too.

Chapter 20

☆ ☆ ☆

True Confession: I hate nicknames. They never tell you anything about who a person really is.

I'M SITTING IN THE CAFETERIA WITH MY TWO BEST friends, Alyssa Grace and Kelsey Taylor, at our usual table in the corner. They don't notice me staring at them. They're too busy arguing over which movie to watch later. Tonight, after Alyssa is finished with rehearsal for the spring play, we're going over to her house for a sleepover.

Winston Academy lost Groove It Up. Once everyone finally stopped dancing, Zack asked Justin and me to stand center stage. When the judges announced that American River won, I shook Justin's hand and quietly slipped off the stage. Kelsey and Alyssa were waiting in the wings for me, armed with brownies and cheesecake. That next Monday, Kelsey's first day back at school, Melinda and Jenna went out of their way to let everyone know they thought it was my fault Winston lost.

When Kelsey and I entered the cafeteria, we saw Melinda and Jenna sitting at the Court. Melinda was still sitting in Kelsey's seat.

"You know what's going to happen if I go over there," I said to Kelsey. "But you can go without me. I'll be okay, really."

Kelsey stared at the Court for a moment. "No," she said finally, "I think we're both done there."

Kelsey found us a corner table, and when Alyssa came to get her lunch, she sat with us. Now Alyssa eats with us a couple days a week. Sometimes Kelsey and I hang out with her in the Dungeon. And sometimes—when the door to the practice room is locked, and no one else is around—Kelsey and I rap with Tasha and Dominique. We're terrible, but they don't seem to mind.

It was pretty rough that first week after the competition, especially the night when Shattered Stars performed at American River. But after the first couple of weeks, most people left me and Kelsey alone about Groove It Up. And the ones who didn't figured out pretty fast that, whether she's queen of the Court or not, it's a bad idea to mess with Kelsey. Not unless you want a very long and very public tongue-lashing.

I joined the Academic Smackdown team. Bethany Perkins says I'm the trendiest AcaSmacker she's ever seen. Last week we went to a meet against American River and we slaughtered them. It was awesome. Especially since I beat Justin every time the two of us faced off on a question.

I never signed up for Camp Colonial, but I am going to Boston in the summer. I convinced Mom and Dad to take a week off work so we could go on a family vacation, the first one we've taken in a long time. And if we're feeling really crazy, we may even leave our cell phones at home.

"We need a plan for high school," Kelsey is saying to Alyssa now that they've finally decided on a movie.

"Not this again." Alyssa groans.

Kelsey has been busy plotting her entrance into high school. Besides making the varsity soccer team as a freshman, she's decided she needs to become the president of the student council. Kelsey figures if she wants everyone to know her name, she should go into politics.

"It's only March," Alyssa points out. "We still have a few months left in middle school."

Kelsey waves her hand dismissively. "Middle school is old news."

While Kelsey and Alyssa bicker, I glance over to the Court. Melinda sits at the head of the table, nodding regally as Derek offers her a soda. Word around campus is that Melinda and Jenna are requiring the Court girls to wear hats on Fridays. But no one except Kate Newport seems to have listened. The three of them are wearing matching weird pink-and-silver hats that, in my opinion, make them look like court jesters. Kristy catches my eye. She glances at Melinda and Jenna, rolls her eyes, and waves slightly. I smile and wave back.

After Alyssa and Kelsey decide they'll discuss Kelsey's plans to conquer high school another day, Alyssa glances down at her plate of chicken enchiladas. "I hate cafeteria food." She looks up at me. "Did you bring us any samples today?"

I pull a container from my backpack and open it. "I call them butterscotch vanilla muffins."

Kelsey sniffs the muffins suspiciously. "You didn't put anything weird in them, did you?"

"Not this time." I've started working on my own cookbook. I've even given it a title: *Polly's Peculiar Portions*.

I finger my heart necklace while I watch Kelsey and

Alyssa eat. I've been wearing mine lately. Every now and then Kelsey and Alyssa wear theirs, although I think they do it just for me. It feels like old times. And I know it might not last. But I know something else, too. I know next time I'll be prepared.

On the day Kelsey and Alyssa and I first broke up as best friends, I felt like I had two choices: follow Kelsey to the Court or Alyssa to the Dungeon. It never occurred to me I could have picked option C: neither of the above.

I know there may be a day in high school when Kelsey will seek popularity (again) and Alyssa will refuse to come along for the ride. No matter what path the two of them may take, I'll always root for them. But now I'm ready to find *my* path. No matter how bumpy and twisty that path is, I'm going to love it. Because it will be my own.

It's funny, but now that I'm not popular, no one ever calls me Plastic Polly. They just call me Polly. And that's the way I like it.

Acknowledgments

As I wrote this book, I thought often of the friendships I treasure in my own life, so thanks must first be given to my incredible Journey Girls: Ann Davis, Cara Lane, Carrie Diggs, Ruth Gallo, and Sarah Mahieu. The five of you give me the space to be the real me, and you love me anyway. Every woman should have friends like you.

To those who read early drafts of this book: Doug Coleman, Ruth Gallo, Lisa Allen, Nancy Winkler, and Stefanie Wass. I treasure your feedback more than you could possibly know.

To Kathy Boyd Fellure, for the perfect plot point at the perfect time. To my husband, Ryan Lundquist, who spent hours on a rainy Saturday afternoon dreaming up "True Confessions" with me. The best ones are yours!

To Elizabeth Thompson, Joanne Kraft, and Chris Pedersen for your wisdom and guidance. To Xochi Dixon, I walk on your prayers. To Shannon Dittemore, you are my BWFF!

To the Apocalypsies, and especially to the Words of Wonder authors: Anne Nesbet, Jenn Reese, Marissa Burt,

Laurisa White Reyes, and J Anderson Coats, you have all made my first year as a published author a lot less scary, and a lot more fun!

To Kerry Sparks, Alyson Heller, and Team Sparks, for your incredible encouragement and support.

Thank you to my friends and family and to everyone else who has read my work and cheered me on, I feel incredibly blessed to have such a fantastic support system.

And finally, thanks must be given to my two sons, Noah Robert and Thomas Austin. The world is a better place because you're in it.

Be sure to check out *Seeing Cinderella*
by Jenny Lundquist

☆　　☆　　☆

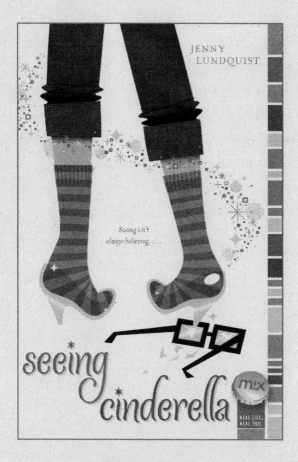

✬ ✬ ✬

Super Freaky Glasses Rule #1
*Don't get upset if someone secretly thinks
your glasses are ugly. They are ugly.*

PACIFICVIEW MIDDLE SCHOOL REMINDED ME OF A SCIENCE experiment gone wrong. A maze of gray metal lockers snaked in all directions, making me feel like a lost lab rat. Six hundred other rats also crowded the halls, some looking as nervous as I felt.

Ellen and I had been blessed with two classes together: math for first period and drama for seventh period. Just thinking about drama made me want to barf, but I figured I was really lucky to have two classes with my best friend.

I found my locker without too much trouble. After that, I needed to run an errand for Ellen. She wanted to join the yearbook club. Since my locker was closer to the English hall, she said it made more sense for me to pick up the application. Applications, actually—Ellen wanted me to join too. Ellen's goal was to throw herself into middle-school life. She thought we should join as many clubs as possible, which was a serious problem for me. Because my goal was just to survive middle school. By being as unnoticeable as possible.

Even if I didn't plan on joining any clubs, I was happy to pick up an application for Ellen—if I could just get my locker open. But after ten minutes of spinning, twisting, begging, and pleading with the attached combination lock, my locker sat smugly shut.

"What are you doing at my locker?" said a rough voice behind me.

I spun around. A pale-faced girl with midnight-colored hair glared at me. She wore all black. She also wore a dog collar. Really. Around her neck hung an actual dog collar, black with silver spikes.

"Um, well." Visions of getting stuffed in a trash can, locked in a janitor's closet, and a number of other scary images ran through my mind.

"I *said* what are you doing at my locker?"

"Th-this is my locker," I squeaked.

"No. It isn't." The girl shoved her locker assignment

slip in my face. "I've been assigned to three twenty-three. This is number three twenty-three."

"I know, but there's a shortage. So they had to double up on some of the lockers. It says so right here." I pointed to her slip.

She looked at the slip, rolled her eyes, and glared at me. "Mess with my stuff, and you'll be deader than the Doberman who used to wear this." She tugged at her dog collar necklace. Then she shoved past me and started spinning the lock. After five spins, three nasty words, and two punches, the locker finally sprang open.

While I waited, I fished my shaking hand into the plastic baggie in my jeans pocket and popped a couple of Red Hots (my favorite snack when I'm nervous) into my mouth. Then I unzipped my backpack and looked for my locker slip. Maybe by some miracle I was at the wrong locker, and I could just walk away from this angry girl.

My hand closed around my glasses case and I figured if there was ever a moment when I needed to see clearly, this was it. I put my glasses on, grabbed the locker slip, and noticed two things. The first was that the words were *a lot* sharper than when I read them earlier this morning without my glasses. The second was that the slip *did* say locker 323. Rats.

I popped a couple more Red Hots into my mouth. Their cinnamon smell didn't cover up the stinkosity of the hallway, which reeked of floor cleaner and sweaty gym socks.

Then something totally weird happened.

I'd heard about people hallucinating when they're stressed out, but this was worse. Way worse. All of a sudden, the air became wavy and shimmery, and computer screens the size of textbooks appeared out of thin air and hovered next to each student in the hall. Something that looked like a commercial played on one screen. On another, white words scrolled across a blue screen like those tele-prompters newscasters read from.

My mouth dropped open and I felt dizzy from staring at the screens. I stepped backward to get a better look, and collided with a group of students.

"Hey, watch where you're going!"

"Outta the way, Curly," said a boy who'd smacked into my shoulder.

"Don't you see the floating computers . . . ?" I said, staring at the strange screens.

"Move it," said my locker mate from behind me.

I turned around, and read the words scrolling across the screen hovering next to her:

Why is that four-eyed loser staring at me? I still need to find my class. At least it's just gym. No reading. I freaking HATE reading.

"How could anyone hate reading?" I asked, mesmerized by the screens.

Her gaze narrowed. "I didn't say I did. And what's the matter with you? Are you stupid or something?"

I stepped backward, bumping into even more students. Soon I was surrounded by a sea of people staring at me like I was captain of the freak squad.

Not that I could blame them. Normal people don't see floating computer screens in the halls of their middle school.

"Those glasses are, like, seriously geeky." I heard one girl whisper to another.

"Is everything all right?" A man who looked like a teacher waded through the crowd.

"What are your names, young ladies?"

"Callie Anderson," I said, while my locker mate answered, "Raven Maggert."

"Well, Callie and Raven, we don't want to start a fight on the first day now, do we?"

A screen appeared by the teacher's head and words scrolled across: *What horrid glasses. What were her parents thinking?*

It was the stress, I knew it. Middle school and my dorky glasses were a deadly combination.

"Anyway," the teacher was saying, "the bell is about to ring. I suggest you all move on and get to class."

"No problem." I slipped off my glasses, shoved through the crowd, and ran away.

First period hadn't even started yet, and already people thought I was a weirdo.

Ellen had her nose buried in a flyer listing Pacificview's extracurricular clubs when I arrived in math class. She didn't look up when I sat down. "What if we joined the hall monitor club?" she said. "We'd get to know a lot of people right away."

"Sure we would," I answered in a shaky voice. "They'd get to know us too—and run the other way."

I looked around the classroom, but didn't see any floating computer screens. Maybe if I took a few deep breaths and ate a few more Red Hots, I wouldn't have any more hallucinations.

"That's ridiculous. Only the slackers would run the other way." Ellen looked up then and frowned. "Are you okay? You look totally freaked out."

"I think I'm having a nervous breakdown."

"Will you stop with that?" Ellen said, sounding annoyed and going back to the flyer. "It's just middle school."

"No, that's not what I was—"

"And anyway," Ellen continued, "you can't spend another year hiding out with your journal. My mom says it's a new year and we should open ourselves up to new experiences."

"I don't care what your mom says. And I don't need new experiences," I said, thinking of the floating computer screens and the way everyone stared at me in the hall. "I like things the way they are."

That wasn't true. I didn't like things the way they were now. I liked them the way they were two months ago. During the first half of summer Ellen and I bodysurfed at the beach and had sleepovers at her house. We ate pizza and watched movies until Tara, Ellen's older sister, would leave for her dates. Then we'd sneak into Tara's room and read her diary.

Then in early August, Ellen went with her family to Yale—some college where my dad said the blood ran bluer than the Pacific—to get Tara settled for her freshman year. Ellen came home grouchy. I figured she just missed Tara. But every time I suggested we go bodysurfing or snooping in Tara's room she said I was being ridiculous. Everything seemed ridiculous to Ellen lately.

And I had a feeling she would think *I* was ridiculous if I told her I'd just seen computer screens floating through Pacificview's hallways.

"Hmm . . . there's a guitar club," Ellen said.

"*You'd* join a guitar club? Do you even own a guitar?" I didn't mean to sound all rude, but that didn't seem like a club Ellen would join—one that wouldn't win her any awards or look good on a college application.

Before Ellen could answer, a woman with wispy gray hair hushed the class. She introduced herself as Mrs. Faber and began to take roll.

"Calliope Meadow Anderson?"

"Present," I said, ignoring the giggles I heard whenever my full name was called. I glanced at the clock, and started to relax. I'd been in class for almost five minutes and hadn't had another hallucination. Maybe everything was going to be okay.

Or not. After roll call, Mrs. Faber went all drill sergeant on us and said she wanted to find out, and I quote, "how much mathematical data you retained over the summer, if any." So she passed out a practice quiz. Personally, I think that sort of behavior should be illegal on the first day of school.

I put my glasses on, stared at the test, and cringed. Because the amount of mathematical data I had retained over the summer was approximately zilch.

After the test, Mrs. Faber went over the answers and I

kept my head down. If I was seriously lucky, I answered two questions right. I skipped the other twenty-three. But Mrs. Faber seemed to have that special superpower that helps teachers zero in on students who are totally lost. "Could you tell us the answer to problem two, Miss Anderson?"

And then, it happened again.

As I looked up—about to give some bogus answer—the air waved and shimmered, and a screen appeared next to Mrs. Faber's head. Inside, blinking in bright pink neon letters, was the number twenty-nine.

I took my glasses off and rubbed my eyes, certain I was headed for the loony bin. But when I looked up and stared at Mrs. Faber, the screen had disappeared.

Quickly, I slipped my glasses back on. There it was: the screen next to her, with the number twenty-nine inside. I took my glasses off—the screen disappeared—and polished the lenses with the bottom of my T-shirt. Then I slipped them back on. The screen appeared again, the blinking pink twenty-nine inside.

So *I* wasn't a freak after all. My glasses were.

"Are you catching flies, Miss Anderson? Close your mouth. Now, does anyone *else* know the answer? Yes, Miss Martin?"

"Twenty-eight," Ellen said.

"No."

There was a gasp next to me—Ellen was probably shocked she'd actually gotten an answer wrong. Then a thought so fantastic occurred to me I nearly fell out of my seat. And I figured, *why not?* So I raised my hand.

"Yes, Miss Anderson?"

"Twenty-nine?"

"Yes, dear." Mrs. Faber smiled. "The answer is twenty-nine."

No. Freaking. Way.

The rest of class was the same. Mrs. Faber asked for an answer and I'd see a number on the screen hovering next to her. Whenever I took my glasses off, the screen disappeared. But as long as I kept them on I could see the screen that held the answers to Mrs. Faber's questions.

Maybe I was going crazy. But I figured if I was going crazy, I was going to do it in style. I raised my hand for every question, and when Mrs. Faber called on me, I had the right answer, courtesy of my super freaky glasses. Who knew having the answers could be so much fun? Not dreading it when the teacher called on you. No wonder Ellen raised her hand so much.

"And finally, number twenty-five?"

"Thirty," I called, and by this time my voice was confident.

The bell rang then and the rest of the class scurried off to second period. I gathered my things slowly, enjoying what was probably a once-in-a-lifetime experience.

Ellen cornered me as soon as I stepped out the door. "How did you know the answers?"

As Ellen asked the question, the air shimmered, and the screen appeared next to her. Only this time instead of numbers, there were words inside. Lots of words.

White letters scrolled across a blue screen: *There is no way on earth Callie could've known the answers to those questions. I bet she cheated off me. Maybe that's why she gets good grades in English. Maybe she's a cheater.*

"I am not a cheater!" A few students heading into Mrs. Faber's class turned and stared.

Ellen paled. "I never said you were a cheater."

The words on the screen changed: *Did I say that out loud? But she's right, I guess. Something's definitely up though. Callie stinks at math.*

"Did you pick up the yearbook club application for me?"

I blinked and tore my gaze away from the screen. "What? No. I got distracted."

Ellen expelled a puff of air, and the words in the screen changed again: *Figures. I swear, I should've just picked it up myself.*

I stepped back in surprise. Were the words on the screen Ellen's *thoughts*?

"Callie, are you okay? You're acting really weird."

"I'm fine," I said. I decided to perform an experiment. "What do you think of my new glasses?"

"They're nice," Ellen said.

But that's not what the screen hovering beside her said: *They're hideous. They make your eyes look huge and your teeth look even bigger than they already are.*

"You don't think they make my eyes look big?"

"Don't be ridiculous," Ellen said. But the screen said: *Yep, big as saucers.* "Look, I'm going to be late. I'll see you in drama, okay?" Ellen hurried off, and the screen beside her disappeared.

I stared after her, frozen. My glasses had magic powers.

They could read people's thoughts.

Real life. Real you.

Don't miss any of these **terrific** Aladdin M!X books.